THAT TIME I DID A FAVO(
WAS ALMOST BUGGERE(
DEMON D(

(A Working Title)

By Donnie Rust

JAKUB

You are one of the good ones
don't ever change broheim.

Donnie Rust 16.12.16

I would like to state for the record that everything in these pages is absolutely true.

Ever lie in bed and find the darkness soothing? Like a peaceful silence for the eyes. Then, other times you lie in bed terrified of every shadow; certain that something has wrapped itself in them and is staring out from them, waiting for you to fall asleep.

As a boy there were some nights I was certain that I would die in my sleep, positive that I would become one of those victims of an uncertain ending. Certain that I would serve only as a tertiary character in a prologue of a horror novel, a means to introduce a wicked and horrible monster to the plot.

I had spent most of my childhood believing I was not the main character in my own story. I assumed that such nonsense would vanish over time and that such self-engineered mind games would dissipate with adulthood.

Unfortunately, the only thing that adulthood has brought is the absolute certainty that there are a good many things lurking and leering patiently in the shadows.

ONE

The girl was talking at me again.

I replied, "Do you know that there is a distinct moment when you realise you've grown old? It's the moment when loud music in public places bothers you."

The girl couldn't hear me over the music, but with great persistence she shouted something that sounded like, "Whathootenay?"

I smiled. You know the type of smile. The kind of smile that every man who wears a suit and sits in the VIP lounge of the biggest nightclub in the city drinking champagne uses when he knows a woman can't hear him. It's a smile that says, "I've said something splendidly clever and you missed it – aren't I so attractive in my suit?"

It is the sort of smile that when you use it, you feel superior but when you see someone else use it, it makes them look like a douchebag.

The girl sidled closer to me on the sofa and draped a long slender arm behind my shoulders so that she could lean into my ear. I've seen this manoeuvre many times in films. In films, nightclubs like this always have music which is *just* at the right volume so that people can converse without getting a sore throat. But of course in films the music is added later and the actors are acting, and even the people dancing are dancing in silence. She got so close to my ear that I could feel her hot breath on my earlobe.

"I can't hear what you're saying!" she shouted at the top of her lungs a centimetre from my ear canal.

Her piercing Essex accent dulled the heavy drumming music into silence. I recoiled and replied, "Gods you stupid cow, I'm not deaf!"

I stuck a finger in my ear and gave it a good wriggle and could hear the sucking-fleshy sound that such gestures make and realised, a few seconds later than I should have, that the music had stopped.

1

"Sorry," I apologised to the girl, who sat on the sofa staring up at me with a bemused look on her face.

She pointed at her ear and shouted, "I can't hear you over the music you stupid bastard!"

The VIP room had transformed into a fish market, where the sounds people made under the blanket of loud music filled all the available space without any cover to hide them.

The irregular, out of time tapping of fingers on the bar and tabletops from the table in front of us was juxtaposed against the off key, ear-shredding singing of people 'getting into' the music. In the booth next door someone was letting off an outrageous fart, and when I peered over the top of the seats I found a gaggle of women sipping cocktails noisily as if they were drinking them through their noses. One of them had a big pink inflatable penis floating about her from a strip of twine tied around her plump wrist. Incidentally, she had also cocked her hip.

"Oh look at you standing there trying to look all superior," the girl said by my side, smiling and looking out into the crowd like a lioness surveying a herd of slow-moving zebras. It wasn't the Essex accent, I decided, but rather her use of it – she could have had any accent, from Irish through to Tanzanian, and she would have been able to make it sound like a handful of marbles being ground together.

I smiled gracefully at her and pointed to her half empty glass of champagne.

"Oh I'd love a drink, thanks babes!" she said with enthusiasm and took up her glass to empty it while I made my way to the bar. As I departed I heard her say after me, "You'd better be rich, you cloot!"

I could feel the music vibrating through the floor and my chest, into my very bones, but I couldn't hear it. I positioned myself at the bar next to a couple who were shouting into each other's ears and made eye contact with the barkeep.

Instead of speaking, I made the universal sign of champagne, and when he didn't understand I pointed at the bottle on the shelf and said, "That one."

2

The barkeep turned around to collect the bottle and when he turned back he had changed.

Now, you may be wondering why I wasn't worried that I was going deaf or suffering some kind of psychotic break. Truth be told, I live in Norwich. The club was in Norwich, which is in Britain, in Norfolk, one of the major cities that exists upon the pregnant eastern side of the island. A city protected from the rest of Britain with fields of patchwork farmland. To the rest of Britain, Norwich is a "Fine City", and was one of Lord Nelson's favourite cities, but most people don't know its dirty little secret. A secret that I knew, and in knowing was susceptible to these sorts of things with numbing frequency.

The barman had undergone a metamorphosis from a young twenty-something with narrow shoulders, massive spiky hair that looked like a helmet covered in porcupine quills and a waistcoat into a man in his forties – balding quite badly but with enough tattoos and shoulders for it not to matter. He'd become so tanned that he shone in the dim lights, with one green eye and one blue eye and a nose that had taken so many beatings it was just a knot of flesh. He put the champagne bottle onto the bar and calmly said, "Hello Donnie."

"Hello," I said in return, shoving one hand into my trouser pocket while keeping the other on the bar. I tapped my ring against the glass a couple of times, sizing the man up. I calculated that I could probably take him in a fight, but that it would hurt. "I take it you're the one causing this nice degree of silence?"

At that moment a woman to my left broke out in the fakest laugh I'd ever heard. It made me cringe with embarrassment. I looked back at the barman, reasserting my question with a glance.

"In a manner of speaking," he admitted. "But I'll warn you... when it stops it'll hurt your ears."

"I have no doubt," I said, looking around to see if there was anyone else in the room who could be listening. To my left were big one-way glass doors that opened onto the remainder of the club and a writhing orgy of dancing youngsters, blazing in staccato strobe lighting. "So what's up? I'm assuming this is a professional meeting?"

"Oh yes," the barman said. "You're not really my type."

He reached into his pocket and produced a stylish black envelope and put it onto the bar beside my bottle of champagne. He drummed his fingers, which were under knuckles that resembled little tortoise shells.

"A love note?" I asked.

"An invitation," he corrected, using a dishcloth to wipe away a nearby spill. "You've got another party to attend tonight, at the behest of Madam Thankeron."

My hand froze on its way to the invitation, and my fingers curled inwards into a fist in an attempt to distance themselves from the invite. "I'm not going."

The very large barman seemed nonplussed. "You've been invited."

"I have to decline," I said. "It's too dangerous."

"You have history."

"That's exactly what I'm talking about," I said. "You can't make me go."

"Well, you're right, we can't," the barman agreed, tossing the towel aside and folding his arms in front of his chest. Between his wrists and his elbows, muscular coils of snakes writhed beneath the flesh. "But we can wait, Ambassador."

"I'm patient," I said.

He smiled. It wasn't a pleasant smile. It was the smile of someone who knows he will get his way one way or another, and was looking forward to his options. The smile of evil big siblings world over.

There was a reality about Norwich that most people living there didn't see. There is a one way system that makes it difficult to get out if you don't know how. Drivers have been lost within it for hours, going round in circles and just coming back into the city centre. Few people realise the one way system has nothing at all to do with the roads. If he had wanted to wait, he could have literally waited for ages.

4

I sagged. "But I'm just getting into my night," I said. "And I have a girl over there I'm trying to get back to mine."

The barman peered over my shoulder. "Skinny fake blonde, fake breasts, fake tan with the make-up applied with a shotgun?"

"That's the one."

"Looks like you've lost her."

I looked over my shoulder and saw the girl had left my booth and was talking to a group of guys, if you can call it talking. I could hear her shouting from across the room, and the guys shouting back. That their conversation made no sense proved they couldn't hear and didn't care what the other was saying. One of them gave her a douchebag smile and I seethed with anger.

The barman's smile broadened, but while his face seemed quite pleasant all things considered, his index finger landed with a resolute thud upon the envelope and, swearing under my breath, I slipped it into my jacket pocket.

In a colossal explosion the music hit me from all sides, not so much music as just a booming noise. I steadied myself on the bar and looked up at the porcupine-headed young barman, who was looking at me expectantly.

I took out my money clip, gave him some notes and left.

"How's your night going then?" the taxi driver asked me as my seatbelt clicked into place. It was such a prompt question I wondered if he would have asked it at all if I hadn't obeyed the BUCKLE UP sign on the back of his seat.

"Oh, you know," I said, looking at the invitation. "The party has just begun."

"I bet," he said. "Where to then?"

I leant forward and passed the invite over. "Do you know this address?"

There was a second, brief but pertinent, where we shared a conspiratorial moment. "Yeah... I know where that is," he said.

I settled back into the chair, slipped the invite into my pocket and looked out of the window as the driver pulled away from the curb and left Prince of Wales Road.

Chances are, for you, for now, Norwich is a Fine City. Tiny when compared to sprawling metropolises such as London. Picturesque in its beauty, the city is built around a castle – this was for a long time a dysfunctional prison, on top of a hill overlooking two opposing cathedrals of opposing faiths. Those stone monuments of architectural mastery rise out of an ocean of rooftops like cliff-steeped islands. On the map you can walk from one end of the city to the other in an hour. Naturally as all cities do, it is growing; expanding into the residential cascades that surround it, but even so, it isn't what anyone would call a big city. What people don't know about Norwich is that it has more than the map can show. Like a map that has been crumpled up, much more of the city sits in a much smaller boundary line. Along with the city geography, time is also just as distended and twisted.

The roads leading up to Madam Thankeron's estate were no different to normal roads. Lined with buildings with pavements busy with people, they looked like normal roads as soon as you were on them – the only difference was that normal people couldn't find them. But that was the case of all cities; you could spend a decade living in a city and find a road you'd never been on within spitting distance of where you lived.

Occasionally the taxi would take a corner where there hadn't been one, turning onto another road where you were certain there was a brick wall before. Buildings unfolded as if out of a pop-up picture book, and space was crushed, but when you were there it all looked normal.

They say that some parts of Norwich City hide, and it's true. In fact the city is probably larger than London and Edinburgh put together.

By the time the driver took a sharp left and heading up a long cobblestone driveway lined on both sides by tall exotic trees, it should have been dawn. But time as well as topography was crushed and crinkled here. There were still several hours left before the sun rose which served a number of Madam Thankeron's guests just fine.

There is no such thing as a movie-style vampire, which is something worth remembering when one is biting your neck.

The driver brought the taxi to a halt outside the tall, gothic gates. For a moment both he and I marvelled at the size of them.

"I'm not taking you past them," he said. "This is as far as I go."

I fished out some notes and handed them over.

"I've never liked secret societies," he said. "They're always so... so..."

"Secretive?" I asked, stashing away my money clip.

He nodded, his eyes on those dark gothic twists of metal. "Yeah, secretive. How're you getting back?"

"I'll call a cab I guess," I said.

The driver shifted noisily in his seat and brought out a dog-eared business card. He handed it over. "Give me a buzz when you're ready. Some of the drivers are a bit hit and miss round these parts."

I took the piece of cardboard and read it. "Cheers Keith, I will."

Keith accelerated away from me and was around the corner before I had taken a couple of steps. Left and right, the estate wall – a tall gothic tangle of steel – stretched like a cage up and down the street, while on the opposite side of the road there was a line of houses that were all facing away. Just their brick backs faced me.

I buttoned up my suit jacket and walked to the gate.

"Who are you?" it asked.

I held up my invitation to it and from a deep pool of shadows a grizzly hand extended. Long fingers with an extra joint, each the colour of a corpse, reached out and plucked the document from my hands.

"You late?" the owner of the hand asked.

"No," I said. "I'm invited."

There was a mumbled response from the shadows, a sound of a stamp being applied and then the invitation was returned to me. "You can walk directly up to the house. I would not advise going off the path, *Mister* Ambassador."

The gate creaked open, with a long accentuated moan that I felt was purely for dramatic effect.

The driveway leading up to the big house was more of a corridor between two walls of shadows, lit at the barriers by regular electric bulbs like those from the sixties. The amber bulbs gave little orbs of light that revealed the walls beyond were made of trees. Outside the light the shadows were less a matter of light and dark, but more something involving liquids. It was like Moses had parted the waters of some great ink ocean.

I walked as casually as I could up the drive, ignoring the sounds of things moving in the thick brush and foliage on either side. There was the sound of insects, which is usually reassuring in a forest, as long you don't mind your insects being large enough to bring down cattle.

I had never been to the Thankeron Manor before and was surprised to find it was a modern building. Instead of turrets, stone walls and gargoyles it looked like an architect had been given a hundred sheets of glass and steel and had made a giant house of cards, and then thrown in some complicated cantileverage to boot. When books get piled on top of each other they form the same sort of precarious stability, and that's what I immediately felt.

Surrounding the house was a circle of lawn with grounded floodlights casting an upward blaze upon the pale building. Modern music roared and hundreds of people behind the glass walls and out on the patio around the heated pool were chatting and drinking and generally having a very pleasant time. As the manor was one of the highest households in Norwich it overlooked the entirety of the city, lit up by the preternatural night.

A remarkably tall man in a slender black suit with a very, *very* narrow face appeared before me and touched the tip of his top hat in greeting. "May I see your invitation sir?" he asked, in the kind of voice that you hear in your bones.

"I already gave it to the bogeyman at the front," I said, handing it over nonetheless. It was one of those conspiratorial gestures.

The slender man smiled, and it was not a kind smile; his teeth were so straight and perfect it made me think of difficult mathematic equations. "I see the gentleman is familiar?"

I introduced myself properly.

"Of course," he said straightening up severely to his full height, which made me crane my neck. I fought down the expected urge to flee as he continued, "I believe Madam Thankeron is expecting you. How kind of you to fit us into your very busy schedule."

"Us?" I said. "Did Madam Thankeron say why I was invited?"

"Are you not the Ambassador?" the slender man asked.

"This seems more like a social occasion," I said as he led me up the grey marble steps to the front door. "Aren't diplomatic occasions arranged in advance?"

The slender man smiled again, a gesture I wished he would stop doing, but said nothing as he led me into the Thankeron Manor.

"Wow," I said.

I had thought it had been a trick of the light or maybe just a reflection off the surface of the large pool outside. Only when I got inside did I see the single largest aquarium I had ever seen in my entire life.

The interior walls of the hallway were one seamless moulded shape of reinforced fibre, holding in thousands of gallons of water that shimmered aquamarine blue and cast shadows and after images of fish and aquatic wildlife living within throughout the interior space.

The slender man stood in wait with his hands clasped in front of him for a minute or two as I stood with my hands in my pockets, gawping gormlessly at the marvellous aquarium. It extended beyond the hallway, and I suspected there were tunnels leading into other tanks in almost all the rooms. Madam Thankeron had always been a patron of dramatic gestures.

He politely cleared his throat and beckoned for me to follow him.

"Madam Thankeron has asked me to bring you directly to her," he said as we walked down a corridor and then another, past room after room of people in expensive clothes drinking expensive drinks and laughing and chatting.

"Social or diplomatic, this seems to have brought the most interesting of people together," I remarked as I followed him.

The back of the slender man's black suit was tailored to fit, and revealed the fellow's thorax and emaciated waistline. He looked like an insect and moved with a flowing grace that made him look like something out of a slow motion nightmare. Again he said nothing. Silence often gives a more descriptive answer.

We walked up several flights of stairs, past floor after floor of people dancing, chatting and drinking. The night was already several hours in and if this had been a mere human party soon people would be discussing going into the city for some clubbing, or pulling out the drinking games to see who could handle a 'real party'.

The stairs ended at a polished wooden landing that had no banister, which opened onto a delightful five storey drop to an indoor pool below, in which shapes that were *very* large for an indoor aquarium swam. At the far end of the landing was a dark redwood door.

"Madam Thankeron awaits inside," the slender man said, standing with his back to the wall and motioning with a long, sweeping movement, like an executioner's arm bringing down an axe.

I passed him gingerly, my whole body tense with the expectation that he was going to push me over the edge, and I only relaxed a little when I put my hand to the doorknob.

"The gentleman does not trust me?" the slender man asked, as the smooth panel of pale of his face, devoid of eyes or nose save for that smiling mouth, still managed to stare at me.

I cleared my throat. "I am just not ready for a swim just yet."

He smiled again and did not move, or stop smiling, until I had stepped beyond the door and closed it behind me.

I was on the rooftop of the house now, which was not necessarily where you may expect it to be. The sky was awash with more stars than I had ever seen in my life, caught in a three dimensional glory that was too vast and thick for me to properly comprehend. There was no moon in sight, but the Milky Way gave so much light and colour that it was difficult to take my eyes away from it. I could still hear the music from the rest of the house but it sounded very far away and there were other subtle differences that I could notice. Like snowcapped mountains on the horizon.

The rooftop was entirely bare except for a thick Persian rug, on which sat two arm chairs. In one of them lounged Madam Thankeron.

My heart didn't stop at the sight of her – nothing as dramatic as that – but you would be utterly heartless to not feel some sort of emotion when seeing her. She was, after all, a Lilith. I felt empowered, sure of myself and overconfident. I approached her and was halfway from the door to the chairs when shadows leapt across the floor and from them, as if the shadows were black paint and had suddenly drawn them into existence, two hounds appeared. That is, if you can call them that – each was the size of a rhinoceros and reeking of ash.

"Volka, Jetson," Madam Thankeron said. "Heel."

The hounds gave me a warning growl and dissipated into swirling clouds of black smoke that repeated the sound faintly as I walked through it.

Madam Thankeron was a tall woman with jet black hair tied up in a bun and light brown skin covered in detailed red tattoos, which ran from the sides of her face down to the tips of her toes and her fingers. Dressed now in a light blue silk dress that made me think of mummy wrappings, I can assure you that those tattoos covered every inch of her body with swirling symbols, shapes and long forgotten words. Her eyes were the bluest blue and her features so refined that she was one of those people you just stared at without realising.

"Good evening Ambassador," she said formally.

"Hi," I said, holding up the invitation. "You called?"

With a slow, graceful motion, she gestured for me to sit down and I waited for a couple of seconds to test the waters. I wanted to make sure she wasn't using any influence on me before taking the seat that was obviously saved for me. When I did, I found the seat to be a little less comfortable than it looked. Quite low, it meant I wouldn't be able to get out of it quickly if I had to. I may as well have been lying in a hole.

"How have you been?" she asked, speaking in familiar.

"Not bad," I said. "A lot of smiling lately. How about yourself? Haven't heard from you since we last met."

"Do you mean our date?" she asked with a one-sided grin.

"If you call it that. I ended up in the hospital," I reminded her. "And I still have sciatica. Is that how your culture dates?"

She looked up at the stars. "I have no culture," she said. "And your culture has far odder rituals."

"If I was invited here simply for a debate on your sociocultural anthropology—"

"It would be a theological debate, surely?"

"—I will have to leave. I was only instructed to attend the party. Nobody said for how long."

Madam Thankeron took the point. "Forgive me Ambassador. You're right, there is more that I need to discuss. I have a favour to ask of you."

"That is was what I was expecting," I said.

The slender man was grinning when I closed the door behind me.

"Madam Thankeron has said that you are welcome to stay for as long as you like, Ambassador," he said. "And that I should make you feel as comfortable as possible."

I could take a hint. She wanted me to leave.

The slender man followed me to the front door, occasionally passing the greetings to the other guests that I would not impart. It wasn't that I disliked any of these guests, but my mind was on another matter entirely.

At the door the slender man said, "I look forward to your return Ambassador."

"I'm sure," I said back.

"In case you find yourself in need," the tall figure said, slipping a hand briefly within his jacket, before he handed over a neatly made card with a telephone number on it, "I would like to offer my services for any future endeavours you may find yourself engaged in."

I nodded and started down the long drive again. This time it seemed to take longer than before.

TWO

"Mr Ambassador."

The voice became part of my dream, which was odd because I was dreaming that I was having sex with a drum kit that kept changing colour. To this day I still wonder if it was significant in some way. The bass drum was talking to me in a very formal fashion considering what I was doing to it.

"Mr Ambassador?"

I was awake a second or two before opening my eyes and, with them closed, I could tell that it was light. I hadn't moved but was wondering if anyone could tell that I wasn't asleep.

"I *know* you are awake, Mr Ambassador."

Peeling the eyelids back, the sum of the morning light struck me in the head like a hammer-driven eye-pick, and I threw myself away from it with a cry. If I had been in my own bed this would have been limited to a rather dramatic roll over and I would have pleasantly gone to sleep, but I discovered when the bed ran out beneath me that I wasn't, and my cry extended into a scream as I rolled off the edge of the world.

A threadbare carpet broke my fall and I lay staring blankly at some mothballs under the counter while getting my bearings. They were an evasive lot. With the hand not pinned beneath me I patted around my body, starting with my torso – buttoned shirt, suit jacket – and then my legs... ah good, trousers were still on. I wriggled my toes and felt the tight, confining embrace of my shoes. So apart from the demolition crew going ape in my head and the taste of a bear's tail in my mouth I was in pretty good nick.

Above me a face popped into view. "Mr Ambassador?"

"Just a moment," I said, my tongue moving like a dehydrated sock inside a catcher's mitt. "I'm just inspecting the jagger-balleets."

"I beg your pardon?"

I reached out with an arm, glad to find a hand with all its fingers attached to the end of it, and flicked some of the mothballs idly. "Yes," I said to myself. "These jaggers are just fine."

I dusted off the hand and rolled onto my back. Looking up, even through the bluish-purple haze of post-drunkenness mid-hangover, I spotted the pretty face framed by short hair, which in turn was framed by a vast domed ceiling.

Where the hell was I?

"What exactly are jagger-balleets?" she asked, looking down.

"Well that depends on who you are I suppose," I replied, hauling myself to a sitting position, where I waited for my stomach to catch up with me.

"I don't understand," she said.

"I meant, who are you?" I asked, climbing up a shelf stacked with files to my feet.

The woman looked human, which meant and means nothing. Lots of things *look* human. Politicians and vegans are a prime example. She was not unattractive but she had the look of someone who tried to make herself look bland. Her brown hair was cut short, shaved at the back and sides with a bushy fringe that looked boyish. In essence, it did accentuate the slender length of her neck. She was dressed in a mottled black and grey one piece dress, together with tights and professional shoes with slight lifts at the heels. Wire framed glasses with hardly any ocular magnification shielded piercing grey eyes and it looked like she seldom saw the sunshine.

"You're staring," she pointed out.

I shook my head, groaning. "Sorry, my eyes got stuck. Erm, who are you Miss?"

"Beebe," she said. "My name is Vanessa Beebe."

"Are you human, Vanessa?" I asked.

"Last time I checked," she said, adding, "Why?"

"Well, in that case a jagger-balleet is just something I made up to hide the fact I apparently was asleep on this library counter."

She nodded slowly. I noticed she was armed with an iPad and held it like a priest might hold a Bible. This did wonders for her breasts, which were covered by the high necked dress; I realised I was staring again. "You called me Ambassador?"

"Yes."

"But you're human?"

"Again, yes."

"Do you know what I am Ambassador of?"

"Fairly certain," she told me.

"Fine," I said. "I need coffee before we talk."

She seemed okay with this idea. I looked around the library. It was early and there wasn't anyone inside, and the corridors between the tall shelves were empty, but even the spines of the books looked at me with judgement.

"Also, do you know how I got here?"

Norwich, as much as it is a map of a world scrunched into a ball, has one solitary element that has been nailed down onto the wooden desk of reality, and that is a coffee house on Upper King Street. With its wooden timber floors, exposed iron girdles and steel and wooden furniture, it strikes the perfect chord for steampunk coffee chic, and while the standard of coffee draws in people from across the country, it is its value as a sanctuary that has made it very popular for everyone who has ever dipped their toe into the murky pool that is Norwich's underbelly.

The tables were little more than four wooden slats secured in a wrought frame of welded iron, with aluminium scaffolding poles sawn off and reshaped by the hands of a competent metal worker. Unoccupied, the chairs were tucked neatly into the tables so that their upper edges were pressed against them as if they had shuffled there themselves for security and peace of mind, like penguins huddled together in a storm, or fragile chicks hiding next to their mother hen. Given that the chairs were pieces of wood braced together with metal braces and big, bold bolts, it gave them the look of a crippled child held together in shape by splints. It gave them a bravely adorable quality.

These clusters of furniture families sat in a room with plain white walls that held shelves of old books and empty, dusty bottles of antiquated alcohol and framed newspaper front pages of old and new history. Here was a headlined "Man's 'Giant Leap'" from the Evening Bulletin in the 60s, depicting three captioned images from Neil Armstrong landing nimbly upon the moon's surface. There was a large front page of the New York Times during the early decades of the last century depicting the ill-fated Titanic, and here was the caption of Jessica Ennis' miraculous win at the 2012 Olympic Games from the Sunday Times.

These captions of framed history looked down at the furniture and upon the floorboards, which were old scaffolding planks, with hammered-in iron braces to keep them from splitting. They were secure enough to ensure that nobody would ever fall through these thick boards, but had enough gaps so that any loose change would fall through as surely as drops of water through a net.

The different shades and colouring of the wood gave the middle floor of the coffee house the radiating warmth of autumn shades. Everything whispered of history and a past. Each of the floorboards bore the scratched, knothole scarring of a lifetime already spent bearing the weight of loads of bricks, with the perfect half-circle stains of paint cans, the overlapping shapes and ridges of objects that had been spray-painted on them to protect the ground or floor beneath. The warped corners of some of the boards that had been forgotten and left on the scaffolds for too long whispered stories like the elderly men and women crowding the polite, sterile cafeterias of old-age homes across the countryside. They whispered them to anyone who would care to listen, grateful for the opportunity to be useful, to be heard if not listened to.

The chairs and tables, milling about like emaciated cattle at rest, beckoned for weary backsides and elbows to rest upon them, knowing that their presence in this warm, sanctified location was entirely dependent on their ability to offer the simplest of supports.

Upon each table stood an emptied brown bottle from a varied number of alcoholic brands, each holding an orange paper rose. These immortal sentinels with their permanent blossoms and stoic colouring stood watch over their herds, like shepherd's dogs. Ever watchful and ever caring.

From the ceiling hung lightbulbs, shaded by polished black shades that cast spacious circles of yellow light upon the assemblage like steampunk stars in an artist's daydream. Irrespective of the weather beyond the broad bank of windows that overlooked the busy Upper King Street of Norwich, the atmosphere in here was always warm.

It was a difficult atmosphere to capture in words. For some customers, the atmosphere in Aroma could only be described as the first time they visited a truly gigantic library and that immaculate peace that can be found in finding a corner that is surrounded by towering shelves of books on all sides, each title promising adventure and escape. For others they claimed it was like a Sunday morning curled on a sofa in front of a good old, long movie with a happy ending. Despite Aroma not possessing a kitchen, one customer insisted his impression of Aroma was waking up to the smell of bacon being sizzled on a gas cooker on camping trips. More than average said it was like receiving that first proper hug from someone you love with all your heart and miss. A soldier said that his first coffee at Aroma reminded him of returning from war and being met at the door by the running tackling embrace of his St Bernard-Husky cross and that his final cup of coffee at Aroma would feel like the day he had left in the first place.

Also, they double shot all of their coffee so even their lattes came with a running kick of caffeine.

"Are you feeling better?" Miss Beebe asked critically as I started on my second cup.

"Marginally," I said. "How is your decaf?"

She shrugged a shoulder, which is the accepted answer for a decaf coffee. It doesn't even warrant a shrug from both shoulders because, like decaf, that would involve too much commitment.

Halfway through my latte, I put it down onto the saucer and straightened up in the seat, rallying with gusto. "Now then," I declared. "Time for business. What can I help you with?"

"That's quite a dramatic recovery," Miss Beebe said. "I guess a man in your position must be quite accustomed to pretending not to be comatose from alcohol."

17

"It is a skill that establishes itself early on," I said.

And it was a practised art. I had checked in the bathroom mirror downstairs to observe the state of my hangover. Thankfully my eyes, if a little glazed, weren't bloodshot, and my hair, which was kept short so that when it was scruffy it looked styled, didn't have any foreign material sticking out of it. It meant that I was able to give my face a quick wash from the basin and make use of the secret stash of deodorant that the owners kept hidden in a cubby hole behind the sink. Indeed, if you were a loyal enough customer to know where the cubby hole was you were allowed to ransack it whenever the need arose. The coffee shop was owned by a friend of mine and they even kept a spare shirt for me, rolled up in an air-tight plastic baggy just for these occasions. Within five minutes of arriving I still felt like shit – but at least looked polished.

"Are you certain you are okay to continue?" Miss Beebe enquired. "I realise that I have arrived unannounced."

I held up a hand. "You did me a favour. If you hadn't arrived I would have been escorted from the premises by security," I said. "And yes, I'm ready. I've already paid for half a dozen coffees so they'll just keep them coming until I vibrate my way through the floor."

A polite smile told me that flirting was off the table for this one. I relaxed a little.

Putting the iPad flat on the tabletop, Miss Beebe ran her finger across the screen and opened up a folder. "I assume, as you haven't asked what my purpose was, that you were testing me?"

"Sure," I lied.

"I am from the Norwich City Council," she said. "Special Branch. I know that you were invited to Madam Thankeron's house last night. I need to know what was discussed between the pair of you."

I took up my coffee and finished the last half of it. I could feel the caffeine taking effect and reminded myself I would have to eat something soon.

"I am not at liberty to discuss it," I said.

"But you are human," she reminded me. "Surely you know where your loyalty lies?"

18

It was my turn to smile politely. "Loyalty doesn't factor into it at all. We are all citizens of Norwich City and I attended a party where I could act as Ambassador. There is nothing to discuss."

"Is it because the city doesn't pay you a wage that you are so prepared to keep the secrets of outsiders?"

Whereas earlier I had stared for an entirely different reason, this time I stared out of disbelief. It was a long enough stare to determine whether she was bluffing or straight up playing some sort of joke. I was disappointed to find she was serious.

"They were here first, Miss Beebe," I said. "We are the outsiders. And yes, that is as good a reason as any why I am employed as the Ambassador between them and you. A mediator."

"I guess I shouldn't be surprised that you're interested only in money," she said.

"I did not apply for the position," I said.

"But you take the money happily enough," she pointed out. "Although you hardly seem to take it seriously. If we were to pay you, would you tell us about the meeting?"

"It was a party," I said. "I shared stories about tennis matches and drinking games with some diplomats. Nothing to tell that would interest the likes of you."

She took a deep breath. It had the same effect as a run up. "Mr Ambassador, you must know that Norwich City balances on a knife edge – and that the other side is trying to tip the city towards them. There are simply too many shadowy areas in the city that need to be brought into the light. Information is the one thing that matters now and we need as much as we can get. Madam Thankeron represents one of the powerhouses of that world and you owe it to your species to share with us the secrets she may have imparted to you. It's your obligation to your humanity, your responsibility. Your mouth is hanging open."

I shut it, blinked, shook my head, and accepted the coffee that the waiter brought over, drank some, put the cup down on the saucer and asked an obvious question. "Are you mental?"

"How do you mean?"

"You're asking me to be a spy!"

"I'm just asking you to tell me what she told you."

"That's what you'd ask a spy to do," I pointed out. "No. I'm not doing it. Despite your opinions on me and the fact that I can't remember the few hours leading to you finding me in the library, I know what I am meant to do. How did you find me there anyway?"

"CCTV cameras saw you going in," she answered. "But not coming out."

"Special privileges I guess," I said, asking an unasked question.

"Indeed," she said in answer to it.

"I'm not playing spy for you."

"Then our interview is concluded."

"*This* was an interview?"

"Well it wasn't a date."

As she stood and left I yelled after her, "Who thought this was a date?"

THREE

What is seen can never be unseen. The scientists at CERN discovered this a few seconds after switching on the Large Hadron Collider. I imagine that they thought, "This is historic and we will never forget this moment!" – then the Hellspawn of Lethiamagori arrived through the dimensional portal that they had opened.

It's impossible to see the world in the same way after your eyes have been opened, which has a habit of baring everything you are to the brazen light of reality. It was something that plagued my mind as I walked home.

On the surface, Norwich is a scrapbook cityscape with a myriad of different architectural styles shaping it.

But, walk past a building every day and never stop to ask what is inside it, and when you're invited there one night you discover that there is a forecourt garden inside the size of the state of Texas. When you first discover this it is a big *truth*, but it is overshadowed somewhat paradoxically by another truth, in this instance being that I could see the same building from my living room window and that it stood behind the garish yellow lights of a Jet petrol station and the worst kebab shop in Britain.

"Hiya," a cheery voice called from behind me.

Not turning away from the window, I replied with a quiet, "Hey."

"Oh, I'm sorry... are you being stoic?" my housemate asked.

My shoulders drooped. "No," I replied, somewhat too soon.

"Because I can leave and let you get on with it?" Nikita said, bustling around with a basket of laundry. "I know how much you love to monologue when you're alone."

I scowled. It is near impossible to maintain any pretence with a housemate, especially one who occasionally has to haul you into the recovery position when you've passed out on the living room floor, but as I had fought off two of her ex-boyfriends when they'd come knocking she didn't tease me too much and I continued to tell her lies. Nikita was the owner of Aroma, and therefore one of the most prized creatures in the city. She also believed that she was just human, but anyone could have told you otherwise – human, Lost or Late.

"I don't monologue," I said.

"You're using your monologue voice," she said, kneeling in front of the washing machine. I didn't say anything for a moment, but the spell was broken. I slumped into my hammock and swung idly, with my legs dangling over the front. Eventually Nikita realised I wanted to say something and stopped with her domestics long enough to give me her attention.

"I have to be back at the shop in like ten minutes," she said. "So out with it."

You had to be careful with Nikita. She believed she was human and that she lived in a human world, but her body knew otherwise. Every now and again, for example, her natural long straight blonde hair would blow out away from her face despite there not being any wind, and her eyes could catch the light in just an *otherworldly* kind of way. Both things happened at that moment.

"You first," I said.

She made a clucking sound in the back of her throat and went back to ramming her laundry into the washing machine like someone punching a pillow. I watched as her hair curled up at the tips. She slammed the washing machine door shut and twisted the dial so sharply I flinched. Crossing her arms over her chest and leaning back on the kitchen counter, she glared at me from across the living room.

"Is it *that* obvious?"

"I live with you. I know when something's happened."

"It's nothing worth talking about."

"Holy cow, this is serious," I said, swinging out of my hammock (...I did not swing. Nobody can get out of a hammock easily, most people believe it's got something to do with physics and the design of them but it's because all hammocks are magical. Lie in one on a summer's evening and tell me I'm wrong).

"It's Reginald."

My brain panicked. Nikita was not someone who had a lot of boyfriends. It was simply that I am a very self-involved person and tended to forget the details about other people's lives that don't directly impact me.

"Oh yeah?" I said.

Her face blanked for a moment. "Really? Really big guy. Bigger than you? Reddish brown hair?"

"I know who Reginald is," I said gruffly. "What is up with him?"

"He hasn't... you know?"

"Nikita, I'm not a woman so I don't pick up on feminine cues as well as you think..."

"He hasn't... you know...?"

"I think I might know," I ventured. "But I will warn you I've had a pretty odd morning so far."

"He hasn't tried to shag me yet."

"Oh," I said, the word literally escaping my lips. "How many dates have you gone on?"

"Four," she said. "And they've been great. He's a real gent and I know he likes me because I've seen him looking at me... like that..."

"Is he gay?"

"No, he's been looking at my tits and my ass enough to not be gay."

I didn't have the heart to mention that meant nothing. Nikita could turn gay men straight faster than a four ton hydraulic press could straighten a coat hanger. I floundered. "Maybe he's a gentleman?"

But I knew that wasn't true. Again, Nikita had that *presence* about her and besides, gentlemen were the most uncommon species in Norwich.

"Maybe," she said, and looked up at the ceiling as the cycle started.

I rocked back onto my heels. "At least he hasn't forced himself on you," I said. "Because you know I'd have to step in and sort him out."

She smirked.

Nikita Hood came from a large family of very large men and dainty women, all under the impression they were entirely human. I was the Ambassador standing knee-deep in two different pools of strange and I was petrified of crossing them.

"If he's taking his time it's not a bad thing," I said, deciding I was dealing with something outside of my realm of understanding. "Maybe just give it time."

"Maybe. Now who was that nerdy chick you were with at the coffee shop this morning?"

"That would be Miss Beebe," I said. "It was business. I think."

"Well, she's geeky with glasses... kind of hot."

I had other things on my mind and hadn't given it much thought, but I suppose she was attractive in a librarian kind of way. I drifted over to the fridge and took out a carton of orange juice and drank from it, while Nikita played with a lock of her hair at her jawline, unbeknownst that the hair at the back of her shoulders was dancing in response. I handed her the carton and wiped my mouth. "What are the plans for tonight?"

She chugged down the remainder of the juice and tossed the carton into the trash. "Well, funny you should ask, Reginald was going to come over if that's okay?"

"You live here, Niki. You don't need to ask permission to bring your boyfriend over."

"He is not my boyfriend."

"Fine," I said. "But whatever Reggie is, he is welcome here. I'll make myself scarce."

"Don't call him Reggie," she warned, walking down the corridor to the door. "He prefers Reginald."

"Really?"

"Yes!"

"You sure he isn't gay?"

"He'll be here at eight, so be nice!"

24

FOUR

I had an extremely hot afternoon bath and woke up, looking like Ken Barbie in water that had turned colder than those found in the Arctic. Shivering, I towelled myself off and had a shave. I felt better than I had, but the hangover was lingering in my subconscious like the eyes of a crocodile lurking on the surface of the water, watching me and waiting for an opportunity. I forced myself to eat some steamed vegetables and sat on my sofa, laptop in my lap, scrolling through emails and social media updates. Then I played my guitar for a bit, watched some TV, even fired up the old Xbox. Anything to stop me from thinking about what Miss Beebe had said about my loyalties.

I did not like being criticised by a member of the Norwich City Council, for whatever reason, but reminded myself that none of the Otherwise of Norwich had ever caused me as much trouble as I had been caused by the human hooligans who poured out of the football stadium on a Saturday. In my mind the Late/Otherwise of the city, for all the legends, myths and stories, were more peaceful than any human.

I was engulfed in my game when there was an unexpected static hiss from behind the sofa.

My body acted by itself and threw me off the couch just as from the cushions there exploded a stack of six foot needles of black glass. I hit the other sofa with my shoulder and swung my laptop, which my hand had somehow found, up in front of me, saving me from getting a faceful of the same needles.

The computer was ripped out of my hand and smashed against the wall by a ragged tendril of coiled fabric, which led back to a Needleman.

"Who sent you?!" I bellowed.

In response the Needleman recoiled its tendril into the man shape of wrappings and fabrics that concealed the creature within, like a mummy's bandages. The long needles withdrew from the

25

cushions of the sofa. Nothing happened for the longest moment and I actually believed that the assassin was going to answer my question.

It seemed to take a brief but resolute breath.

Cursing, I scrambled to my feet, dived headlong over the armchair and rolled across the floor as the chair was perforated by a wall of needles that slammed through it and into the kitchen counter. Wood splintered and coffee cups shattered whilst I rolled to my feet and sprinted across the kitchenette and down the corridor shouting, "You stinking stack of laundry, that was an authentic custom-made Chesterfield!"

I leapt to the left, ducking behind the wall of Nikita's bedroom and colliding awkwardly with the bathroom door. Plaster exploded over my head as needles as fragile looking as crafted glass but as hard as steel punctured the corner of the wall above me.

"You clearly know who I am!" I called, looking all around for anything that I could find as a weapon. "So I will give you ample and fair warning, if you leave now you'll leave alive!"

The needles rattled together as they were withdrawn, but the Needleman did not venture down the corridor and I couldn't see its shadow in the rectangle of light that was thrown down by the late afternoon sunlight coming through the hallway. But I knew in my guts that it had not left.

What were the chances that Nikita would have anything in her room I could fashion into a weapon? I rattled the door handle open and fell backwards into her room.

The reason I never went into Nikita's room was because of her presence. As this was the place where she slept it was the place where her smell was strongest and it hit me like a pillow to the face and threw me for a second. It took a couple of slaps in the face to clear my head.

Bedlinen, clothes strewn across the floor, drawers overflowing with lingerie, colourful socks and beads, jewellery drooped like tinsel around a wooden carving of a tree. Open cupboards thick with dresses and collared shirts and scores of shoes pouring out like bricks from a bombed building – and tucked away in the corner

26

between the wall and cupboard, with scarves wrapped around the hilt, so casually leant up there that it was almost invisible, was an iklwa spear.

The Needleman was at the door, testing it, rattling it, but hesitating to come into Nikita's room.

It knows who I live with, I thought, taking up the short spear and testing its weight. The two foot wooden shaft was perfectly balanced to the one foot long broad spearhead. It was not a weapon made for demonstration or praise. The shaft was wound tightly with bindings at the top, middle and at the neck around the blade. The blade itself was sharp where it needed to be but the metal was pitted and well used. This was a weapon that had seen much blood.

The rattling of the door stopped and I braced myself out of the way of the door, anticipating another needle attack. I counted my breaths for a full minute before I dared go to the door.

I cracked it open an inch and peered out into a sunlit corridor, where plaster dust floated lazily through the sunlight amongst the chunk of wall now scattered across the carpet. I opened the door wider and risked a peek out.

Static erupted behind me, and even though I flew out of the room a piercing hot pain shot out of my right bum cheek as one of the needles gorged its way in. Using the iklwa I cut at the tendril holding it and scrambled across the corridor into my room and kicked the door shut.

Wincing, I gripped the needle and ripped it out of my bum cheek, seeing the thing turn to ash in my hand.

Another static hiss directly above me, and I rolled to the side just in time to avoid a storm of barbed needles that bore into the carpet. As gravity drew the Needleman to the ground beside me I slashed out with the iklwa, feeling the bladed edge scour against something within the mess of twisted fabrics. There was a hissing screech of pain and the assassin wheeled away from me. Sweeping smoothly to my feet, I took advantage of its retreating steps and attacked with the short spear in hand, my kali stick training swiftly coming into play. *Keep control of the centre, contact with the target isn't enough to cut; you have to guide the blade.*

Sparks flew from the spearhead as I collided with whatever was beneath the laundry, but I wasn't going to get caught in a fight with something that out-weaponed me. So as I attacked I scooped the corner of my duvet from my bed and, keeping in stride, I threw it over the assassin and ran for the window.

Swearing against the pain in my rump as I mounted the desk, I tore open the window and looked back just in time to see my duvet turn into a comet's tail as a dense tree trunk thick column of needles exploded towards me. I grabbed the blind above the window and in the same moment jumped off the sill. The blind caught the needle attack, which missed my scalp by centimetres, and slowed it down enough for me to slam the window shut.

Choking on ash, I picked my way across the roof tiles to the edge where I used the rain gutter to get down and dropped into a dumpster.

From there I limped to the main road and ran in front of a Skoda that had accelerated to catch the lights, causing the driver's eyeballs to pop out of his head as he yanked the steering wheel to the side. The ensuing calamity of screeching car tyres and bellowing car horns was lost on me as I stood in the middle of the road with my hands covering my face. When I dared look I was surrounded by stationary cars with very angry drivers getting out. In that stunned silence between accident and preceding the angry rebuttals of the drivers, I looked up at the second floor window of my apartment and saw the Needleman looking down at me. The image vibrated for a second then vanished in a static hiss.

I looked away from the window and one of the drivers who had stepped out of his car shouted something about a weapon and punched me in the snout.

FIVE

Ever since an incident a little while ago, under my bed there has been a shoebox. An ordinary looking shoebox made of white cardboard. I only ever looked into it at the first day of every month when my pay to the exact penny would arrive in bundles of neatly pressed and stacked notes. I knew almost nothing about the payers, only that they filled my shoebox with money at the start of every month. The shoebox was important to me because it meant that to someone, somewhere I was performing a function which meant I was valuable, which meant I was not surprised to hear a tentative knock at the door.

"Who is it?" I asked. It sounded like I said, *"Hoo- ih-it?"*

"Open the door, Ambassador."

Holding the iklwa at my side, I cracked open the door and peered into the blue and green eyes of the barman. "What are you doing here?"

"Maybe I'm here to finish the job?" he said, folding his big tattooed arms across his chest; there were intricate patterns of rose bushes and chess pieces dancing across his giant forearms.

"No," I said, fiddling with the tufts of tissues I had wedged up my nose. "You're not dressed like an assassin."

He didn't move but I had the impression he was waiting for an explanation. "You're wearing a white T-shirt, denims and biker boots." I held the door open to him. "If you were coming to finish me off you'd be dressed more appropriately."

He nodded and leant down and picked up a gym bag I hadn't noticed. He walked past me and said, "No worries. I have my overalls in the bag."

I closed the door behind him and for the second time in twenty-four hours started wondering if I could take this man. He didn't look spectacularly fast, but then again neither was I at the moment, and he looked like the kind of guy who couldn't give up in a fight even if he wanted to.

The barman walked into the middle of the living room, surveying the destruction that the Needleman had wreaked. Once he had done a once over, he put the bag on the floor and zipped it open. I stayed warily away from him, my hand still gripped tightly around the iklwa as he pulled out some green overalls.

"You aren't actually here to kill me are you?" I asked in earnest.

The barman gave me a severe look as he pulled on the overalls. "No Donnie, I am not here to assassinate the Ambassador. You have had some trouble and I'm just here to secure things."

He walked to the windows and looked out at the road where the cars were still clustered around each other, drivers still yelling and arguing. "Why didn't you fight any of them down there?"

"I didn't want to hurt them," I said.

"How very noble of you," he said, going to the bag and taking out a large black candle. "Do you have matches?"

I went to what was left of the kitchen counter and found an intact box of matches in the decimated drawer.

"That's a bit of a scratch you have there," he said, pointing to my rump. "Do you have the needle?"

I shook my head. "It's a Needleman. The needles disappear into ash when disconnected, so there is no evidence."

"You shouldn't let it fester," he said. "Do you know how to treat that?"

"Bleach," I said. "Stings like all manner of hell but I don't think it was poison. You don't send a Needleman to use poison."

Without another word the barman scraped a match across his facial stubble and the flame flared up, but then was drawn across to the thick black candle, where it burned brighter and gave off a hissing noise that, when listened to long enough, took on the sound of whispers.

"Is that a barrier spell?" I asked.

The barman walked along the walls of the apartment, pushing furniture aside as if it weighed nothing and holding the candle flame up to the corners. The smoke rose and spread itself across the edges and nooks, searching and separating into tendrils. There was a hissing noise as they tied together across the ceiling.

"It is," he said. "This is the strongest protection we can offer you."

"Would have been good to have it before," I said, plugging a finger into one of the holes of the counter. "Look at this place."

"I know," the barman said. "But hindsight is twenty-twenty, as they say. We are arranging your protection, don't worry."

"Do you know who I live with?" I asked.

"Everyone does," he said. "But we'll give you some other protection."

"You say we," I observed. "Do you work for the Embassy?"

"I'm a subcontractor," the barman said, moving past the windows with his arms held upright. The candle burned but the wax didn't melt. The whispering grew louder in certain areas and the smoke hung in certain corners for longer before fading into the architecture. It wasn't magic, but more of a kind of Otherwise chemistry, like a trail of salt and alcohol to ward off slugs from your rose bushes.

I moved out of his way as he passed me. "As a subcontractor can you help me clean up this place?" I asked.

The barman chuckled. "I can give you the name of a good plasterer if you like," he said. He went down the corridor with the candle, lining the corners in Nikita's room, the bathroom and my bedroom. With someone else in the room the damage seemed all that more impressive. I checked my watch and a mild panic engulfed me. "She's going to be home in half an hour!"

"Oh dear," the barman said as he walked past me again, making his way back into the living area – it was important to create a complete and unbroken loop. "Whatever are you going to do?"

"I'm going to lie, obviously," I said.

"I think that would be best," he agreed, finishing his loop and drawing a complicated symbol with the smoke before snuffing out the flame with his fingers. He put the candle back into the bag and unzipped his overalls. "Now, Madam Thankeron has asked me to remind you that you are expected at her house again tomorrow morning and that you mustn't be late."

I blinked. "You're kidding. Look at me."

He fished a card out of his back jeans pocket and handed it over. "Go here, it's a good barber shop."

"...Called 'Cut Throats'?"

"Yes, but they are the only ones who'll be able to fix you up in time for the meeting with Madam Thankeron. Now, I'll leave you to clean up this mess."

SIX

"What the hell happened?" Nikita asked, loudly.

"Where is Reggie?" I asked, as innocently as I could while sweeping up the plaster in the hallway.

"No, my question first," she insisted, looking around. All of her hair was curling now, coiling to the scalp like springs readying to be unleashed. It was quite unnerving, giving the impression of a silent countdown. Fortunately I had crafted a story so perplexingly absurd that I was certain she would buy it.

"An ex-girlfriend paid me a visit," I explained, pointing to my swollen and bloody nose to slip in a sympathy card. "She came in with her new lover and trashed the place."

"What the hell did you do to her?" she asked accusingly.

Wow, I thought, she believed that easier than I had expected. It made me step back onto the defensive. "I didn't do *anything*." I pointed at my face again. "She broke my nose!"

Nikita stalked into the living room and swore loudly and explicitly. When she marched back down the hallway there were curls of hair levitating above her like rearing snakes. I held the broom in both hands like a baseball bat.

"They've trashed it!" she shouted, stamping through the flat. "This place is totally ruined!"

Once the barman had left I had taken a look at the full extent of the damage, and it was severe. Several items that Nikita had contributed to the house had been obliterated. She looked far more furiously at me than I had planned and I almost blurted out the truth, but fortunately instead of the truth there emerged another lie. "I know, it was fucking insane. I thought she was coming here to get a booty call and then this guy shoves his way in with a sledgehammer!"

"A sledgehammer?" she asked. "Doesn't look like a sledgehammer did that kind of damage."

"She had a normal hammer," I said hurriedly. "And a screwdriver. I got stabbed in the bum cheek."

"Seriously Donnie – what did you do to her?"

"Oh come on, I didn't do anything to her." (Ironically the only truth sounded like a lie). "She's just a bloody crazy person and her boyfriend's a cocaine-riddled freak."

"Did they take anything?"

"No," I said. "They just wanted to hurt me and break things. But after she stabbed me in the butt they left."

She peeked into her room. "Holy shit, look at my room!"

Maybe I should have invented more than one guy, I thought. She stood in her room screaming for a while and then said the words I was hoping she wasn't going to say. "I'm calling my brothers!"

"Nikita, no!" I said, dropping the broom and putting my hands together. "This is my fault. I will replace everything they broke of yours. I'm sorry."

"Why not? Have you called the police?" she asked.

"No," I said.

"Well *you* said that you didn't do anything wrong!" she argued, taking out her phone.

"Please don't embarrass me in front of your brothers!" I pleaded. "I've called a really good plasterer and he'll be in tomorrow morning. In the meantime I'm going to clean this place up and you go on your date. Speaking of which, where is Reggie?"

"Don't *call* him that!" she shouted. "And he's running a little late. What are we going to do? Our home is wrecked!"

There was a knock at the door and Nikita yanked it open so suddenly that the man on the other side jumped. Her hair fell to her shoulders in a heap. "Reginald!" she said loudly, before correcting her tone, "Hi – err."

I interceded smoothly, pulling the door completely open and smiling at the very big, very redheaded, very inhuman man who had come to meet her. My expression changed suddenly, as did his, as we saw each other.

"Evening," he said very politely.

I unclenched my jaw. "Evening," I replied.

Nikita looked between us. "Do you know each other?"

"No," I said. "Reginald, I'm Donnie, Nikita's housemate. I'm really sorry but I had a domestic today with one of my exes and the place is in a mess."

"Dare I ask what you did to deserve this?" Reginald asked.

I took a deep breath and counted to ten. Nikita said, "Come in Reginald, and see what Donnie's love interests do to other people's property."

Reginald stepped forward and was about to walk through the door when he stopped abruptly just at the threshold. He frowned, his eyes snaking to me, before looking upwards at the lintel. I pressed my lips into a thin line and shrugged.

"What is it?" Nikita asked.

"It's me," I said loudly. "I look like an absolute mess. Listen – why don't the two of you go out tonight? I'll clean this place up as best I can."

"But you look hurt," Nikita said caringly. I would have snorted if it wouldn't have been painful.

"I am," I admitted. "But when Reginald goes mental and destroys the house then I'll leave you to clean up the mess."

"Not that I would!" Reginald said so quickly that she gave him an odd look.

"Go out, go somewhere nice," I said and then, more to Reginald, I added, "And *busy.*"

"Oh, I don't know," Nikita said.

"Go on," I urged. "Go get dressed."

"But my room's in a *state!*" Nikita said again. "Why did *your* bloody girlfriend have to ransack *my* room?"

"That was more her new boyfriend," I said. "He didn't touch the cupboards though, so grab what you want and get changed in the bathroom. They didn't go in there."

She looked up at Reginald, who smiled and said, "That sounds like an idea. I know a great place for food."

Uncertain but willing, Nikita stepped over the broken door into her room. She was muttering ruthlessly.

"*Did you put up the protection because of me, Ambassador?*" Reginald asked, his voice suddenly so many octaves lower it sounded like gravel.

I squared up to him. "No, but at least I know she's safe if you try anything."

"*That's racism,*" he growled.

"It's actually specism," I corrected sarcastically. "But if you mention anything to her about what's actually happened here..."

"*I don't know what's happened he–* Oh, I love that skirt," he said, changing mid-sentence from one tone to another as Nikita stepped out of the room and showed him a skirt on a hanger.

"I won't be long," she said. "For God's sake please come inside!"

"I don't want him ruining his shoes," I said pleasantly.

"They're brand new," he added. "I was trying to make a good impression."

She rolled her eyes. "You guys, always trying to outswing each other. Don't let him intimidate you Reginald."

We smiled until we heard the shower start and I turned back to Reginald. "It had better be a coincidence that you're dating her."

"*I didn't know that her housemate was the Ambassador,*" he replied, rising a couple of inches as he straightened up – squaring up to his full size, I felt my neck straining to look up at him. "*So why would I know what happened here?*"

"Still," I said.

"*Do you think me an idiot Ambassador?*" Reginald asked. "*Is that your opinion of my kind? That we are idiots?*"

I wasn't going to rise to that. "I am trying to protect my housemate."

"*You think I could be a danger to her?*" he asked, and laughed, which had a cavernous quality to it. "*Even if I wanted to harm her in any way I wouldn't be able to. Ambassador, please...*"

His quality softened. Without changing any spatial dimensions he went from being gigantic to being merely tall and broad. From the shape of a monster he became merely monstrous. "I want her to like me."

Abruptly ashamed, I explained — "I can't take down the barrier and my concern goes beyond merely what you are, Reginald. This was an attempt on my life."

"*Assassination?*"

"Well no," I objected, "I am still very much alive so it was an assassination attempt."

"*By whom?*" he asked.

"It was Otherwise," I said, answering the real question. "Not a human. But, that doesn't mean anything. I just want her to be kept safe and out of it, do you understand?"

He nodded. "I will do everything that I can."

"Thank you," I said.

"Also, just so you know, I thought I would take her to Middletons," he said. "Will that be public enough?"

"I guess it's the only place you can get a decent steak, eh?" I joked.

"If you ask for the right menu they will let you go out and kill the cow yourself," he said with a smirk, then baulked. "Not that I would do that of course, Ambassador!"

I held up a hand. "Jeez... call me Donnie."

He seemed pleased with this and remained outside until Nikita joined us, again asking if I was sure I didn't need any help cleaning up. I assured her that it was all in hand, then with a parting nod from Reginald they left. I closed the door and chuckled. Just when I thought the day couldn't get any weirder I discovered Nikita was dating an ogre!

SEVEN

The builder arrived and gave me a quote for the work that had to be done. I paid him a deposit and told him to get started right away. Nikita called me and apologised for her outburst the night before and said that she had spent the night at Reginald's house and that she was almost certain that he was gay.

"Why?" I asked, the phone clenched between my jaw and my shoulder while I changed the dressing on my bum cheek wound.

"His house is *amazing,*" she said. "He's got a garage filled with cars and a Ducati Diablo!"

My heart sank. That was my favourite bike. But there was more. "It's got a massive glass wall that separates it from the rest of the house, which is really unique and spacious. I walked in there and thought... that's it, I'm shagging this man tonight."

"And?" I asked, wincing as I applied more bleach to the wound.

"Well we kissed but he didn't take it any further!" she said. "He was so gentle and respectful!"

"That not a good thing?"

"Not when I want to be shagged!" she shouted down the phone. "Is he gay?"

"Honestly, I don't think he's gay," I admitted. "How was Middletons?"

"Good," she said. "Why do you ask?"

"No reason," I said, tearing off a strip of duct tape and flattening it over the gauze. "I have a morning meeting so I have to get ready. The builder said he'd be able to do the work but it'll be a couple of days yet, I've ordered you a new bed and mattress and it'll be delivered today at some point. That cool?"

"Yeah," she said. "Unless I manage to get Reginald to do the dirty with me."

"Best of luck. Toodle-pip."

I changed the tape across the bridge of my nose and dressed in one of the only suits that were left intact after the Needleman's attack. Black, with a white shirt and a slender pink neck tie, which offset the dark bruised patches under my eyes. I ran some wax through my hair and decided that I looked ready to get some answers.

My phone rang again and showed an unknown number.

"Hello?"

"Hello Donnie," the barman said. "How are you feeling?"

"Not bad," I said. "You checking up on me?"

"Madam Thankeron is as well-known for her patience as you are for your punctuality," he pointed out. "And I have booked you in for a session at the barber."

I had forgotten about that. "I really don't think I need to go to that," I said.

"I feel that it is best that you look your best," the barman said. "So as to not alarm anyone."

I chewed on the idea for a while. "I don't know if I can trust you."

"And I totally understand," the barman said. "The barbers are expecting you at 10AM and Madam Thankeron is expecting you at one o'clock."

"You said something about a guard last night," I said. "What am I to expect about this?"

"Are you wearing your black suit?"

"Yes... I am."

"Power suits are all the rage nowadays," he said, then hung up.

Cut Throats.

Everything of value comes at a price – and for many Otherwise in Norwich, that price is not only about money. The better the service the higher the price, and there were barbers who offered better service than anywhere else and at an affordable price that was simply too good to quaff at. Well, financially at least... but while you lay there, spread out on their barber chairs while they scraped their razor blades across your throat, or while you sat in their seats and they trimmed your hair, you couldn't realise what they were taking from you.

Forget what both science and religion tells you about the soul. It does exist, but it is both more amazing and disappointing than you would expect, and it can be replenished. Because it can be replenished, there are those creatures that have evolved to feed off it, and all they need are willing subjects.

I limped into the barber shop on Elm Hill and was immediately welcomed by a man with a blinding white shirt, shiny cufflinks, a black waist coat and a black tie. His perfectly trimmed hair was matched only by his perfectly manicured hands and his smile could have come out of a catalogue of 'charming facial expressions'.

"You leave my soul alone friend," I said warmly as he took my hand and shook it.

His beaming smile didn't even falter for a second. "Ambassador, how good of you to come. I can see you do need some fixing up. What would you like today? A shave perhaps?"

A cool shiver went down my spine at the thought of anyone with a blade at my throat and it occurred to me that I didn't know who had sent the Needleman after me. "Is there any way we could dispense with the pretence and cut straight to the fixing me up bit?" I asked.

"Haha, you jest," he said, clapping his hands together.

"Sorry?"

"You said 'cut'," he said with an indulgent smile.

"Oh," I said.

"Indeed," the barber said. "Please come with me."

I was led past a row of barber chairs that were occupied by humans enjoying their shave, haircuts and shampoos. All these services were performed by cutthroats; there were no human employees here at all, whereas most of the customers were exclusively human. The barber took me through a door into an adjacent room, which had a comfortable leather armchair and a wash hand basin. He gestured for me to sit down, and after a quick inspection of the chair I did so.

The barber washed his hands and slipped on white latex gloves.

"My name is Andrew," the barber said. "Ambassador, I can understand your reservations, so I will not take offence to your earlier lack of manners."

I felt compelled to explain but he wiped his hand aside and continued. "I completely understand your concern. I can see the injuries that you have suffered and can see what has caused them. The nose was by a human hand but the wound in your buttock was by an Otherwise assassin... you do not trust me, but I'd ask you to appreciate that much of what makes us Otherwise is uncontrollable. Do you notice how your wound in your backside no longer hurts as much?"

"Yes," I admitted.

"That is due in part to you shaking my hand. My kind's touch carries with it a mild anaesthetic, because not only are we barbers and manicurists but we also make excellent doctors and nurses. It's in our chemistry."

"Why the gloves?" I asked.

"For me to fix your nose and to completely repair the wound in your thigh will mean I will need to touch you for longer than a handshake... which would result in some absorption. Fortunately I will be able to heal both wounds with some mild resonance treatment which does not require direct contact. May I fix your nose first to demonstrate?"

I nodded, a little dubiously, but as he reached down to my face and his fingers ever so gently touched the wound I felt a soft vibration, like a physical purr, that went from his fingers into my face and tickled my skull from within. There was an unusual sensation like a very deep itch and a pain, so quick that it was scarcely recognisable at all.

He stepped back, hands spread to the side in a camp 'ta-dah' fashion. I reached up and found that my nose was completely intact. "Unfortunately, there is little I can do about the shape," he said.

"I'm fine with it," I said, immensely pleased.

"Now let me get to your bum," he said.

EIGHT

"Late yet?" the gate asked as I approached.

"Not yet," I answered, watching the taxi drive away. "Despite the best efforts of some."

"What is it that is said about roads and good intentions?"

"Something about paving and Hell I think," I replied, shoving my hands in my pockets and looking for the source of the voice. Beside the gate there was a hole. Not a hole in the wall or in the ground, just a gap, and a shadowy gap that grew the longer you looked at it. It made the air around it look cold. Within the hole I could just see the twisted hair like extensions of roots coming out of the earthy interior curve of a tunnel.

"I think I once saw you under my bed," I said conversationally to the bogeyman.

The gate creaked open and from the hole came a wet chuckle. "No, that was not me."

Walking up the driveway to the Thankeron Estate during daytime is little better than walking through it at night. The difference is that at night the darkness is almost total, whereas during the daytime the light causes trickery between the trees and you can see just how dark and deep the forests are. Above, pale daylight barely seeped through the thick canopy of twisted branches and the dim illumination managed to only enhance how thick the forest was. The tall columns of the trees with their tangled roots seemed to move when you weren't looking and the thick undergrowth, as soon as you looked away, seemed to shift ever so slightly closer.

Norwich was folded up onto itself, therefore so was the forest. If you strode from that driveway and walked in one direction it would take forever to reach the other side. Crushed within the orbit of that estate was hundreds of miles of dense woodland.

As I approached the house I saw it was cast under a gloomy skylight. Despite it being a balmy day with skies of the most majestic blue anywhere in Norwich, in the Thankeron Estate it was so overcast it looked like the marble of the world had been dropped into a pocket of cotton wool.

Like a dorm room on a Sunday morning, the whole estate seemed glazed in a sheet of grey, caught in an architectural hangover.

Nobody was at the door to greet me so I wandered around the front of the property, walking along the tiled walkway leading from the circular turn around at the front of the house. I passed glass walls on my left shielded by heavy black curtains to a pool that looked cold, deep and uninviting.

I was wary of approaching this body of water too closely, recalling a memory of being a child swimming in the pool alone one afternoon and ducking under the water and discovering that a pool of six feet is an ocean without end when you're under it and unable to get to the surface.

The sensation of holding my breath and looking up at a surface, the full panic and the heavy desperation of a body trying to breathe, was so fierce and sudden a memory that it made me stagger away from the pool's edge clutching at my chest.

Preternatural cold shivers raced across my body and I gasped, turned and walked head into a tall slender man in a suit, then screamed so loudly it left me feeling light-headed.

The slender man stooped and picked up his top hat and put it back onto his shiny bald head, whiter than the sky behind it. His pained grin stretched wider. "Have you ever drowned, Ambassador?" he asked.

"No," I answered. "Not in this life, at least. It just looks very cold."

He nodded slowly, his smile making it seem that this information gave him a special kind of delight. "Madam Thankeron is of course expecting you. Please come this way, if you will?"

I followed the slender man onto the veranda, which cut beneath one of the cantilevered floors above, past forlorn outside furniture and into a French windowed entrance. The slender man waited for me to follow him inside, then he slid the door shut behind us and drew the heavy curtains closed again. I didn't like slender men – they were just... off. Just not quite on the right side of a line. There had been a spate of teenage hangings in Britain in 2005 and they had been linked to slender men; or maybe *this* slender man.

He moved past me, so close I felt the air curdle between us. "Please follow me."

"One moment please," I said.

Bodies lay slung across the long, wide furniture and as my eyes adjusted to the dark I could make out their odd movement. Eyes, catching the luminosity of the scant light, glowed as they turned to watch me. The smells of different Otherwise were not unpleasant, just odd, and they made the mind want to seek them out, some out of a desire to find the source and others out of a desire to get rid of it. Nature is all about variety, and not all plants attract insects by being sweet smelling.

"Are we ready?" the slender man asked after a while, now reduced to an almost stick figure shape in the gloom.

We passed under the aquarium and the indoor pool at the base of those banister-less steps. With the lights switched off it looked as deep and as uninviting as the pool outside, and I had the strangest suspicion that they were connected. I saw movement beneath the water of something much larger than what you'd expect to find indoors.

"Follow me sir," he said with a smile and started up the stairs.

We walked to the top floor and strode down a corridor with rooms on either side. The slender man turned and said, "Madam Thankeron awaits within."

I entered a spacious bedchamber with ceilings at least four metres above. It was as long and as wide as a tennis court, and along the entire wall on the right was an extension of the aquarium. The interior lights were turned off, but I saw more movement within those waters.

I closed the doors behind me and took in the other details of the room. The carpeted floor was very deep, so deep that it actually unbalanced every step and was brilliant white. The left hand side of the room was a long bank of black curtains, with only one section opened to let in the daylight and offer some light to the room. It cast foreboding shadows across the chandelier fixture in the centre of the room's ceiling. At the far end of the room was a very large, very sturdy bed; so large it looked more like a yacht. Four double king sizes could fit on that bed frame, which was carved from the trunk of a giant sequoia. The posters were as thick as columns holding up a Greek temple's ceiling and the headboard was a panel of wood thicker than a house wall.

Lying in the centre of it, her black hair draped over her shoulders and her red tattoos obscuring her face but making her eyes blaze, Madam Thankeron waited, a lit cigarette in hand, the smoke passing through the dim light.

"Do not linger in the shadows, Ambassador," she said. "You do that too well for a human."

"I am not lingering," I said. "I am merely staying where nobody can slip behind me."

"That sounds almost like an accusation," she said. "What have I done?"

"It has been a very long day already," I said. "And I have many duties. As much as I appreciate being summoned, I am not at your beck and call."

She brought the cigarette to her lips again. Its tip blazed. She was wearing a royal blue silk nightie. I had seen that nightie before.

"I am certain you are able to spare me a few moments of your time," she said. "I wished to speak of business anyway, so it can be fitted into your schedule I am sure... have you considered the favour I asked?"

"Not fully, but it has caused me a lot of problems already," I said, walking to the left, away from the aquarium and to the curtains. I used a finger to draw one of them back and looked out of the window. I saw mountains with white peaks.

"Important matters will often do that," she said. "What progress have you made so far?"

"It has only been a day," I reminded her. "I don't work that fast."

45

"On the contrary. If I recall properly you were a very fast worker indeed," she said coyly, shuffling across the bedsheets. "Do you remember it?"

"I still have the scar tissue," I said.

"Yes, we play rough," she said.

"Played," I corrected. "You played rough."

She gave a little laugh. "Don't worry Donnie, I'm not here to seduce you. This is just the place where we had the most common ground."

The shadows were thickest on either side of her bed. I walked to the curtains that were open, allowed myself to be safely within the daylight and said loudly, "Volka! Jetson!"

The hell hounds stirred, rising briefly from the shadows before realising they had been duped and sinking into them again. They growled angrily as they sunk. "Do you feel that I am dangerous, Madam Thankeron?" I asked.

She made a tutting sound, discarding the pretence of being an alluring seductress all at once and sweeping herself with maddening speed from the top of the mattress to the side of the bed, where she wrapped herself in a dark shadow from the wall. She walked to the foot of the bed, tying the black silk gown around her body. "There was an attempted assassination yesterday."

"I am aware of this," I said.

"By a human," she said.

Somehow I managed to keep a straight face. "You mean here?"

"By a *human,*" she repeated.

It took a while for the penny to drop. "You think it was me?"

She drew a long drag on her cigarette, the lit end causing her red tattoos to glow. "You do have the training."

"Why would I try to assassinate you?"

"It was not me who was the target," she said.

"Oh," I realised. "It was on the life of the one we spoke about."

"You do have the training and you are the one person who was in the know," she said.

"It wasn't me," I said. "I was busy."

"Doing what?"

46

"Fighting a little prick," I said.

"You need to be gentler," she said.

I let her jibe hang in the air. She picked up on the hint very fast and without a change of expression she said, "A Needleman attacked you?"

"In my home," I added.

"I am not responsible for that," she said.

"I didn't think you were," I said. "If you wanted me dead you'd have far simpler and devious methods of doing it that wouldn't involve something as destructive as a Needleman. Whoever wanted me dead wanted to send a message to everyone associated with me."

"This is true," she said with some measure of pride.

"Your assassin got away," I said. "May I see where the attempt failed? Perhaps I can be some assistance finding who *is* responsible."

"Do you think we need assistance?"

"You thought it was me," I said bluntly. "And it wasn't. So yes, as you've drawn a blank, I do. Now show me."

She strode past me in a whirl of silk fabrics, saying, "Of course. It's time I introduced the two of you anyway. Come along."

For a house of this size it didn't have that many rooms, officially at least. It wouldn't have surprised me to find that the doors to closets and cupboards may occasionally lead down long corridors that were too long for the architecture, but for the most part the house was made up of only a handful of very large, spacious rooms, although you had to check out the windows to make sure you were in the right country.

It was the house of an eccentric *Madame* who preferred glass because she disliked walls and then covered them with the heaviest curtains because the daylight hurt her eyes.

Up more stairs, around more corners, across spacious but darkened hallways where things slept on and around the furniture. Shapes uncurled as we passed.

"Did you have a slumber party last night?" I asked.

47

"Hmm?" she asked, turning her head slowly to the side.

I jabbed a thumb behind me. "People seem to be sleeping everywhere."

"What makes you think they're sleeping?"

I looked over my shoulder. The corridors, with the white plaster walls, were better at using the light, while in the darkness of the other floors you could barely distinguish between furniture and moving body.

"Nothing now," I said. "Are they here because of the assassin?"

"Ha, we prefer to be a little more proactive than that," she said smoothly. The black silk dressing gown had a split from the ankle up to the thigh and her shapely leg kept appearing. Decorated as they were with intricate red tattoos of such precision and taste, I couldn't help my eyes following them up. I fantasised about tearing that gown off her.

A thought occurred to me. "Are they here for me?"

"Yes," she admitted.

"Should I be flattered?" I asked.

Madam Thankeron's expressions were always difficult to read, so I didn't try to decipher them until she spoke. While her expressions were often cryptic and misleading, her words were not. "Do you not think that we would take an interest in what human was appointed as Ambassador between the humans and the Late?"

"I suppose so," I said. "Haven't really given it much thought."

"I see. Have you given much thought to why you have kept the position for so long?"

"I have history," I said.

"Precisely," she said. "You have history. How many lives have you had?"

I blinked but kept my mouth firmly shut.

"Oh don't look so surprised. I know that you have done your best to conceal the level of your schooling and the particular gift or curse you have."

"Sounds like I'm going to have to disappoint a lot of people at some point," I said.

"So says the man who survived a Needleman?" she pointed out. We reached a door, similar in size to the one outside her own bedchamber. She turned to me and pegged me with her bright blue eyes that were far older than the face they looked out of. "Indulge my curiosity, Ambassador. How many Late are here hiding in the shadows?"

"I'm really not in the mood for tests."

"Answer me," she said – then in a far more pleasant tone, "Please."

I fiddled with the buttons at the front of my jacket, then with my cufflinks. Finally, under her expectant gaze, I relented. "Fine. On the bottom floor there are seventeen Otherwise, twelve on the middle floor, eighteen on the third and in the aquarium at least a dozen who are patrolling to make sure nobody got in that way. There are at least six swarms in the shadows and your hounds have been following us as best they can."

She raised a speculative eyebrow with the insinuation that I had over-calculated, but I pressed my lips together. "No. Your nightgown is a shadow swarm and if the carpet in this room is as deep as the carpet in yours then you've also got some weedlings in there."

"And you said you'd disappoint," she said. She turned and put both hands flat against the wooden panel of the door. "Beyond these doors is the subject of our conversation. I won't tell you anything about the assassin as I don't want to distract or give you false clues. How will you want to proceed? Interview first or investigation?"

I shrugged. "It's all happening the same way. But do you really think the assassin is going to make a second attempt?"

"Do you believe the Needleman is going to?" she countered. It was a rhetorical question. "Precisely. Humans are more tenacious than even they give themselves credit for. This assassin has been paid a lot to destroy what is behind this door."

She produced a key and went to unlock it and I took hold of her wrist, stopping her. "Make no mistake, Madam. Just because you are introducing us, that does not mean that I am agreeing to your favour."

My phone pinged with a message, which we both ignored.

"I understand," she said gently, casting her eyes down to my hand. I held it a moment longer before letting go. As she put the key into the lock and turned it I stepped back and put both hands into my trouser pockets. I was very apprehensive. "But before you make up your mind, have a look first."

NINE

"Now you look like a man with a problem," Miss Beebe said when I sat down at the round corner seat at the Cuba Revolutions nightclub. I had only been in the building for less than a minute and already I had a rum and coke in hand.

"Some people collect stamps," I said. "I collect problems."

"Any that I can help with?"

"Not really." I took out my phone and put it onto the table next to the drink, screen up – the universal message for *'You could be a secondary priority'*. "Have you been waiting long?"

"Only since I texted you," she said.

She was using a different gel in her hair today that gave it a wetter, more waxy look. It was a strangely 90's look for someone so young. She had also dressed in denims, cowboy boots, a grey turtle neck and a black denim jacket. I thought quickly about what day it was. "Do civil servants work on the weekend?"

"You do," she said, just as a springy Spanish song was kicked up by the live band, which I had totally failed to notice on my way in. "Aren't you a civil servant?"

"I do not answer to the City Council."

"But you came to meet me?"

"You're hot," I said levelly. "I have a reputation for being a womanising douchebag that I've worked hard to achieve and would like to maintain."

She smiled at me and I could see her brain running through a long list of reasons to dislike me. They made the smile take on an almost venomous quality. I knew that the Norwich City Council had an interest in my affairs and a nervous disposition with regards to where my loyalties rested. I could say that my loyalties lay in the direction of where the money came from, but a shoebox under my bed was not generally a good source for a reference.

"I'm sure you'll do your best," she said, and then with a swift change of tone added, "but I do think we got off on the wrong foot yesterday and would like to try again."

"I thought it was all very clear," I said. "I am not going to be your puppet."

"But you're happy to be a token human paid by a corrupt government?"

"No," I explained. "I said I *won't* be your puppet."

"Their ruling class and the City Council needed to co-exist. To this they need a middle man, someone who could hold the position of *Ambassador*... it is a token position. You don't actually even have a job to do except for meeting with both sides at parties and smiling like an idiot, do you?"

I drank my rum, then held the glass against the side of my head where a small headache was forming. "I love your idea of starting on the *right* foot."

She relaxed a little, but I could tell she wasn't finished. What she had said had been accurate, and maybe I was a token brick in a bridge between two parallel governments, but it was an important brick. It had to be an important brick or else I wouldn't be paid. Unless, of course, I had totally misjudged my position?

Anyway, I had been very honest. I had agreed to meet her because she was hot. I was in need of some fresh company. It is a talent that people think I am usually smarter than I am.

"If you were to share information it wouldn't be spying, because all you would be doing is helping us understand the other side," Miss Beebe persisted. "You would have an actual purpose."

I wet my lips. "You're right, I am the token human who appears at their parties, I sit at the head of the tables at their dinners, and I make appearances and guffaw with the best of them. I speak on behalf of all humanity in matters concerning their world."

"It's ridiculous," she said. "You have no training. No political experience."

"I've learnt on the job," I explained. "Besides, it's much easier when you understand they actually *want* to live in harmony. They just want to understand us."

"Help us understand them too then."

"You don't want *just* information," I said. "You want *specific* information."

"It needs to be relevant."

"Of course it does," I confirmed. "The more relevant it is, the easier it is to follow them... to monitor them. Control them. If I was invited to the Mayor's residence and he spoke with me about certain matters, would it be okay for me to go and share the secrets with the Otherwise?"

She looked angry.

"Besides, are you sure you don't have all the information you need?" I asked directly.

"How do you mean?"

"Are you certain, Vanessa, that you don't have all the information you need to do something incredibly stupid?"

"You're speaking in riddles," she said, picking up her coke and sipping at the straw. "Please tell me I'm not wasting my time."

"Okay," I said, leaning forward with my forearms on my knees and looking across the table at her. "What's in it for me? I'm not paid by the Council, so what can you give me?"

"The knowledge that you're protecting the humans living in this city?"

"I've seen what the humans are like in this city," I responded. "They may have fewer teeth and claws than the Late but they are doubly as brutal. No, you tell me, what is this information worth to you right now? What have you been authorised to give me?"

"We're Norwich City Council," she said. "Not Parliament. We manage the municipality and the logistics of running a city. What makes you think I'm authorised to get you anything?"

"You're seeing me on a Saturday," I said. "You're dressed for a day out on the town, you're wearing a different perfume and you've done your hair. You've been asked to get me on side at any cost and so you're here to deal. Perhaps there is something I do want from you."

I was stepping into shadowy, murky, scumbag territory, but I wanted answers. As repulsive as it made me feel, I gave her a long look from toe to top, making sure that my eyes polished every curve of her body with my gaze. She looked like a woman accustomed to batting away advances by men, but wondered how many were trying to be deliberately despicable. When my eyes eventually met hers, what I saw in her expression wasn't repugnance or rage, but instead an actual willingness, as horrible as it made her feel. A willingness to get what she wanted. In all branches of the Norwich City Council there is not a single agent who had that kind of devotion to her job.

"Or it's personal?" I said.

People look for tics in expressions. I look for blanks – an absence of a tic or tell in an expression that is harder to fake. I sat back, stunned.

"Holy shit... can I see some ID?"

"I didn't bring any with me," she said smoothly.

I threw my glass at her as hard and as fast as I could. It was the kind of gamble that would usually involve a man going to jail – tumbler glasses in restaurants and nightclubs are designed to be handled by drunks. They don't break easily. They're sharp with hard edges, built like transparent bricks.

Yet she snatched it out of mid-air and slammed it down onto the tabletop without a change of expression. It was such a smooth movement that not one ice cube fell out.

A moment paused. We were both counting the people in the club, pinpointing the exits, the position of the furniture and the available weapons.

"I think that is all the identification you need," she said.

I sat back against the cushioned sofa, spread my arms across the top and folded one leg easily over the other. This time I looked at her with entirely different eyes, picking up on all those little details she had been skilfully hiding from me. The school had raised their game since I had left and I was still playing by an old text book.

"You aren't the assassin that they're looking for," I said to her.

"No, I'm the assassin looking for that one," she said.

"Prove it."

"How?"

"What is the assassin I am looking for?"

She caught the attention of the waiter and ordered two more drinks, this time both with rum, and we waited in silence until they arrived. She began succinctly. "Male, under six foot and about seventy kilograms. Makes use of the latest combat suit technology, including nanotech particle blankets to cover his smell and holographic projection to mask his approach... went in two nights ago and waited in one of the rooms. I would wager that he did that because everyone's attention would be on you and Madam Thankeron. He waited on the roof until it was quiet and then climbed in through one of the windows and slipped into his target's location and simply waited until they went to sleep. Then he just took his time. Enough?"

"I guess," I said. "So, why have you been playing the City Council route with me? Why the deception?"

"I wanted to choose an option that didn't have to involve me sleeping with you," she said.

"Ouch."

"Don't be so soft. I cannot stop him if I cannot approximate what he will be doing next. I need to know who the target is – who or what is in that room."

"I can't tell you," I said.

She threw up her arms. "I could torture it out of you?" she said.

"You could try," I said, although a little dry mouthed at the thought. "But I think there is another avenue that you can go through. I was attacked by an Otherwise assassin yesterday at my home."

"They have assassins?"

"Yes," I said. "We had to be taught what we know, but they just have genetic evolution on their side. I got away, obviously. But if you're looking to find out the answers you could start by finding that assassin."

"I don't know anything about Otherwise assassins though," Miss Beebe said. "We're taught how to kill people."

"They *are* people."

"Human people," she corrected. "I wouldn't know where to start."

"Your assassin was going to kill an Otherwise," I said. "Means he had done research, so follow his tracks and see where it points."

This seemed agreeable with her. "Can I ask one question though?"

"Ask it. But it doesn't mean I'll answer it."

"Whatever it is that Madam Thankeron is doing and your involvement in it, it isn't going to be dangerous is it? It's not going to hurt innocent people is it?"

"No," I said. "Shouldn't do."

She paid for our drinks and left. I watched her going, hating myself for how much time I spent watching her buttocks move in those jeans.

When she was out of the door I called the waiter over and asked for a pen and paper, then jotted down the description that Miss Beebe had given me. The truth was I had been so stunned by what I had met behind those wooden doors that trying to track the assassin had completely slipped my mind.

TEN

I went to the gym immediately after and spent an hour lifting heavy weights on bars while glaring at myself in the mirror. Then I spent another hour in the studio pounding the punch bags until I wasn't able to lift my arms any more and my legs were as flimsy as shoelaces.

This wasn't real training for me, in the same way as singers don't practice by hitting those high notes. They practice with bars, with simpler songs.

After this, ten minutes later and I was sliding into the scalding hot waters of my bathtub and putting my head back against the porcelain rim. I am a man in love with bathtubs. A bathtub is the absolute seat of luxury and to take a long hot bath is the height of indulgence in our modern world. Expensive hotel rooms and resorts are measured by their bathtubs and showers in the same way expensive restaurants are by their kitchens and restrooms.

Bathrooms are the last sanctuary in our busy world. A place where you are not expected to answer your phone or be hospitable, it is a place where you can relax and not be called upon to anything.

I felt the tension of the day coming off me in rivulets, vaporising into the air along the tendrils of steam rising from the ocean that surrounded the twin island peaks of my knees. I pretended that I could see faces and dreams in that steam, imagined them shaping. I had once believed that it was a super power, being able to make faces out of nothing. I had believed I had been magic. But then again there was a time when I had believed I was the only person in the world who could see rain and another time where I was absolutely certain I could move things with my mind.

There was the sound of a key scraping the lock at the front door, which I recognised as Nikita's entry and was followed by the sweep of the door swinging shut. It was one of those small pockets of background noise that you get accustomed to when you live somewhere with another person – the sound of the door brushing

57

against the carpet, the tiny creaks on the floor where people walk across their well-established pathways through the house. Nikita had a habit of letting the door swing shut by itself, and I heard the perfectly timed click of the door as it touched the lock.

"You forgot to pay your tab at the shop today," she said, her voice trailing as she went down the corridor.

"Okay," I called back, putting my head back against the tub's rim and bringing the glass of rum to my lips. "You know I'm good for it."

There was an answer, but it was in the kitchen and I couldn't make out the words, just the tone, which was her *'I know, I'm just reminding you'* tone.

I rolled my shoulders and was surprised to hear the popping of the wet knots of my muscles rolling against each other like marbles squealing together in a fist. *You're still tense*, a voice in my head said. *You're tense because you know you're on eggshells.*

On eggshells, that's what my mother used to call it. My mother... my ultimate hero, had lived through the Rhodesian war, had seen her friends raped and bayoneted by jungle terrorists while she hid in the bushes, her hand clamped over her baby brother's mouth to stop the boy from crying out. She had said that most of her childhood was spent living on eggshells, where you took every second for what it's worth and got used to relaxing in the short periods of quiet that happened between the threat of death. "You have to learn to enjoy the scenery while walking through a landmine field," she would say. "Learn to do that while watching your feet and you'll be fine."

My music stopped and was replaced a moment later by acoustic rock. House rules, I thought with a smile. Whoever is able to change the music can. She said that classical music wasn't the kind of music you learn to appreciate when you worked in a coffee shop. Caffeine and classics didn't match up well.

There was still that smell of wet plaster from the repair work on the wall, still that lingering scent of brick dust. The counter in the kitchen was lying in pieces, the contents of the drawers and cupboards piled up on the kitchenette floor. The sofa, which had lain like a felled wildebeest with its guts lying out, had been broken apart and removed but scattered bits of fluff and cushion lay about in the carpet like blood splatters in the grass. If things had been different, if I had been faster or slower by a second either way, I would have been killed. The thought stirred something akin to panic deep inside, where my lungs and heart were connected, which was smothered by something else. My natural ballsy overconfidence.

I drank the remainder of my rum and put the glass onto the floor then, covering my face with my hands, bent my knees and slipped in the water. Any man who's over six foot will know how difficult it is to slide under the water in a bathtub. You bend you knees almost to your chest just to get your face under the water, and it makes you as vulnerable as a baby in the womb.

The hot water poured over my face like a blanket, titillating the nerves in my face and shoulders. I've been a water baby for as long as I could remember, and I love the feeling of my hair waving in the current. I adore the feeling of weightlessness that water can provide, the womb-like quality of it that makes the outside world that little bit quieter, while amplifying the sounds of your own body.

An odd thought, like a 'Did You Know' slip from the inside of a Dylan chocolate bar, sprung to mind – *Miyamoto Musashi, Japan's most famous swordsman, never took a bath because he feared it would leave him vulnerable.*

This was promptly followed by – *You never heard the door lock, did you?*

In a wash of panic I realised that an assassin was standing right over me. Having casually strolled in through the unlocked door, it had somehow managed to bypass the protective charm of the house and, under the cover of Nikita's loud music and even louder cooking, had strolled into the bathroom and was standing over me while I lay prostrated in the most ridiculous position so that he, or she, could see my face, bollocks and ass all at the same time. I was going to die in a bathtub.

Spluttering and gasping, I jerked out of the water to find that I was alone in the bathroom, but the feeling didn't leave me. I reacted as man does when coming out of a nightmare, convinced

59

that his eyes are lying to him and that whatever he was dreaming was still following him. I scrambled out of the tub, sloshing water over the rim and onto the tiled floor, heaving myself into a standing position so that I could face whatever danger was going to present itself.

Tendrils of steam danced and weaved around me, taunting me, teasing me. If they had been able they would have been sniggering. I relaxed, stepped fully out of the tub and sat on its cold rim and took my time breathing in the hot, wet air.

"Get a grip on yourself man," I said.

Another lesson came to mind, this time a bit more welcomed. *Do not stress or worry. An uncluttered mind reacts faster and with better efficiency. Besides, you do not want to die stressed.*

It was a mark of my school. We usually died smiling happily and chilled out. It was the only way to face defeat – armed with a good sense of humour.

Nikita was singing along with her music while chopping something on the chopping board, and I could imagine her swaying and bopping away.

I let out the plug in the bath and took the towel from the hook on the door. I quickly dried myself off and wrapped it around my waist and tucked in the corner. Moving to the basin to run the hot water tap, I sprayed some shaving gel into my hand and applied it generously to my face, my hips swaying a little to the music I could hear. It was awfully steamy in the bathroom. I disliked having the extractor fan on as it had an awful mechanical whirling noise and something was wrong with one of the propellers, because it tended to whistle too. This meant I was walking around in a cloud.

I took out my razor and put it on the side of the sink, washed some of the foam off my hands in the basin and wiped a broad stroke of steam off the mirror.

Someone was standing behind me.

Turning sharply, a dollop of shaving foam flew from my chin and landed with a splat on the most perfect pair of breasts I had ever seen.

"Wow," I said.

She was so beautiful that if she had been walking beside a road drivers wouldn't honk – they'd just drive straight into the car in front of them and die happy. Her hair was blood red and fell around her pale, slender shoulders in a bundle of tousled locks. Her eyes were a glassy green, set on either side of a girlish nose above a wide, petite mouth. The swell of her breasts were more perfect than the swell of soap bubbles caught on the surface of the bath, and as I took my full time looking at her up and down while my mind decided what to do, I can attest that in every way she was utterly perfect. The utterly perfect woman.

I fled.

Or tried to.

With deceptive strength and accuracy she struck out, her open palm smashing into my rib cage as I reached out for the door handle. It made me react instinctively and my punch landed with a sound like a baseball hitting a catcher's mitt as my knuckles hit her cheek.

It damn near took her off her feet, whipping her head to the side and spinning her right round so that she staggered to the side of the tub.

For a moment the only sound was the music next door, then a choking sob from the woman.

"I-I'm sorry," I said.

The woman leant to her right and put a shaking hand to her face. "Why did you *hit* me?" she wept.

"You surprised me," I said. "I don't know who you are."

Let me explain. I'm a six foot five man. I have to have my clothes tailored for me because my obsessive gym training has left me with shoulders wider than most tailors have measuring tape for – *and* as I previously pointed out, I have a *lot* of training. Big guys don't have a lot of options for defence in the eyes of the law when it involves hitting a woman. The words, "But she hit me first," are often not well received. Also, moreso, I was acting on the same character trait that got me expelled from my school. I'm not an absolute bastard.

"Are you okay?" I asked, holding my towel to my waist. She had gotten a pretty solid hit in and my right side was starting to smart.

The redhead's back was pale, the skin perfectly clear, and the movement of her muscles beneath her flesh made me think of wild cats moving in the undergrowth. The piano keys of her ribs shifted beneath the pale skin that glistened with perspiration, and the narrow slip of her waist guided my eyes down to the twin heart swells of her buttocks. As she was bent over the bathtub and not knelt before it, it offered me a glimpse of the delicious folds that lay between those globes.

A feverish itch passed across my face and chest like a towel drawn across it on a hot day and in a dizzying rush it felt like the blood of my whole body dropped into my groin.

My conscious mind was shouldered out of the way by some other monstrous thing that said, *"Take her now... she wants it, can't you tell?"*

Still at the bath's edge, only two feet away from me, she shifted, straightening her legs. My eyes scraped like a razor's blade over the shapely calves, the slender musculature of her thighs up to the detailed crevice of her genitals that swelled with blood before my eyes. From there they went over the round mounds of her backside again, along the sinewy details of her back to the curtain of red hair. She was looking at me over her shoulder, her fiercely green eyes sparkling in the bathroom light. A coy smile on her lips.

The music and Nikita's singing seemed to be very, very far away now and the swelling in my loins had reached an aching point. Her eyes went from mine down my body, appreciatively searching the details of my torso and befalling the bulging tent pole that was holding the towel up. They widened joyfully and her smile grew, causing dimples in her cheeks.

Ohhh, I thought hungrily. *I love dimples.*

"Drop the towel," she said huskily.

The steam was curling around her like scarves being made to dance by incorporeal dancers, and without question I unfastened the towel and let it drop away. Suddenly, with no obstacles, my swelled head, as shiny as a plum, drew itself across the empty space to the tight receptacle between her legs, which had appeared to open as invitingly as a flower to a bee.

62

Think of that wet, deep heat, I thought and my hips gave an involuntary jerk at the idea.

Take, the beast said. *Take her hard. She wants it. Hand around her throat, balls deep inside, slam it hard into every hole until she begs you to stop!*

I longed for it, the feeling of my cock head pressing into that hot, damp entrance, so tight until it surrendered and allowed me full entry and to feel it caress me, embrace and swallow me whole. But more, the ecstatic feeling of her body bracing against me, her gasp as I filled her entirely. That instant where two people became one. The feeling of ultimate satisfaction and connection. Man conquering over all and roaring to the sky as five billion years of evolution culminates in the thrusting motion of his hips!

I stepped in and grabbed hold of her waist and pulled her up to me and bared my teeth in hungry pleasure as she yelped with glee.

I looked down, wanting to see the brief moment of resistance, as the folds of her vagina pressed against the head of my engorged penis and pushed back against it. There is that instant where it distends around the penis head and it's like hearing that perfect high note in a song or seeing a gymnast perform a triple somersault. You just want to see it again and again and again.

But I froze when I looked down. Screamed in utter terror and revulsion. Thrust her away from me, heard her surprised curse as her hands skidded in the tub searching for purpose on the wet interior and the crack of tiles as her forehead stopped her.

I backed away until I was flat against the bathroom door, my hand rattling the door handle, as the eyeball blinked at me from her anus. The puckered flesh of her sphincter moved like a thick eyelid opening and closing around the eyeball, which was green and moved to focus on me.

Eyeball. I couldn't stop thinking of it. There was an eyeball, an eyeball, a freaking eyeball in her ass! I rattled on the door handle again until my hand, by itself, without any command from me, fiddled the door lock open.

The door opened inwards though. The bathroom wasn't that big and even with one person inside it you had to step around the door

63

and the toilet to get out! I pulled it open and tried to squeeze and manoeuvre myself around it without touching her, but before I could get anywhere her leg shot out and kicked the panel of the door and slammed it shut. Her leg bent again and shot out, this time hitting me square in the guts and smacking me back against the door with a resounding thud.

She rounded on me, taking away that horrible, horrible anus eye but presenting me with a visage of her face.

Things had changed. Her green eyes were totally bloodshot, angry blood vessels swarming like vicious red worms around the balls, and she had no mouth. Below that perfect porcelain nose was now just a blank patch of smooth white skin!

She was a shirime!

I had to get out of there.

As she came at me I went fully offensive. You have to fight a shirime as a boxer, not as a grappler or wrestler. *Never* get tied up with a shirime!

As she went low and tried to get within tackling distance, in rapid succession my fists and hands struck her in the face, causing her head to rocket backwards. It was a series of chain punches to her face followed by a meaty hook that flung blood from her nostrils and put her head into a perfect position for an uppercut from the left that felt like I'd punched a bag of dried pasta.

Her hair flinging all over the place, I didn't stop in my attack and kicked her hard in the torso with as much power as I could muster.

But the floor was wet and I hadn't watched my footing.

You never watch your footing!

I was standing on the towel with one foot and the other had been underneath it, so it got caught, and as I kicked I lost my balance and, without a moment's hesitation, she flung herself into the air, tucked into a little ball and kicked out so that both her dainty feet hit me in the chest and hurled me backwards through the door.

Action heroes get kicked through doors all the time in films, so often that it has become symbolic of the hero's ability to keep fighting, but it takes more force than you would imagine to rip a door off its hinges – because as you'd imagine, they are designed to not do that.

Totally winded and my head ringing, I sprawled out across the carpet and, through a daze, saw the shirime rising out of the steam of the bathroom.

Nikita was singing loudly in the kitchen, the door between there and the hallway shut to keep the smells of her cooking from saturating the bedrooms. That was something we learnt about this place after a time when she tried to make garlic bread. But how she hadn't heard this fight so far was beyond me.

"You are a tough one," the shirime said, but her voice did not come from her face, which was still mouthless. Instead it came from another location and from where I lay I could see clearly where that was, and several deep instincts inside me began screaming.

I backed away and hauled myself to my feet, saying, "You ain't seen nothing yet. I'm like old leather, me!"

I leapt in, feinting with a left hook and throwing a right, but she was poisoning me every time I touched her, her skin practically dripping narcotic by this time, and it made my erection grow harder and harder until I was fighting with a flagpole swinging between my hips.

She made several attempts to snatch at it and I dodged, both with skill and luck, throwing blow after blow. That's the secret of fighting. It has next to nothing to do with defence, it's all about punching and kicking and hitting everywhere that will hurt, and fortunately at that moment a lot of that was in the same place. Shirimes kill in a particular fashion, in some countries they were known as the *vaginus tande.*

"Oh you utter prat!" she gasped, her hands dropping to between her legs.

I went in again landed two quick jabs and flung my whole body weight into an elbow.

Years of alternatively striking a leather pad with my elbows until they bled followed by soaking them in salt had created a pad of flesh on each as hard as horn. That's assassins for you... our main weapons are always hidden. Our hands and feet appear positively manicured in comparison to our elbows and our shins. I could smash bricks with my elbows and still be able to play a couple of games of tennis.

The blow struck her right in the middle of her forehead like a hammer swung at pull speed and made a distinct *kgunk* sound.

By the way her head moved I must have broken her neck, yet despite this her hands flew to my sides and, like fishing hooks, dug her nails deep to my sides. Anchoring in.

Together we crashed into the door frame. I threw my weight into her but she didn't release her grip and the barbs in my muscles sapped the strength from my arms. I felt my penis head bump against her stomach and I realised how close we suddenly were.

I used my elbows, delivering blow after blow to her face, but all this accomplished was deepening her grip into my sides. I picked her up, grabbed at her hair, pulled her head back and hammered my fist into the exposed flesh of her throat and brought my elbow down like a guillotine blade. Laughter came from another part of her body, and in response my testicles crawled inside me.

I felt her legs move and managed to drop my hands in time to push her thighs away from me before she could wrap them around me. She was as strong as a fucking ape and was trying to tie herself with me.

"I'm going to take you!" she said, from the corner in between her legs. Her face eyes were glaring at me.

Fuck, fuck, fuck, fuck, I thought.

"Nikita!" I shouted, pushing down her legs as hard as I could as she tried to hook her heels around my waist. "Nikita!"

"Oh bless," the shirime mocked. "Do you think she can even *hear us?* Your housemate is used to ignoring who you shag."

I spun us around and crashed into the adjacent wall, recoiling from her mocking laughter and shrieks of enjoyment.

"God yes!" she cried. "I love it when they struggle. You ready Ambassador? You're about to be inside your last woman!"

It happened without thinking. It's something that every man will at some point do when things get out of hand with an overenthusiastic woman. Usually at the point where a woman has

66

gotten on top and is riding you with unbound enthusiasm, not realising that your penis has its limits. At this point a man's hand will act without thinking.

I reached around her, put my right hand flat against her buttocks, and with my middle finger I jammed it as hard as I could into her brown eye.

Her body jerked in an unnatural fashion, her rear trying to buck away from me while her whole body tensed like a bow yanked on a string. She made a desperate crowing noise and flung herself off me, both her hands flying to her rear.

"Oh you fucking cu–!"

I stepped back, hands up in a guarded position, and with a roar I threw a Muay Thai roundhouse kick into her jaw, which collided with all the power I could muster.

She went from standing to lying down within half a second. Her hair and arms flung out around her, her legs akimbo, she collapsed into a heap of limbs and lay completely still. With morbid fascination I watched as the flesh between her legs rearranged itself like a flower closing up, and a second later the skin on her face shifted and changed to accommodate a mouth, which then peeled into lips and dropped open. The weeping eyeball in her arse drew inside like a critter pulling into its hole and all of a sudden she was just a startlingly beautiful woman lying unconscious and naked in the wreckage of my bathroom.

I shook off my hand disgustedly.

A knock at the door.

"Who is it?" I asked, surprised at the shrill tone of my own voice.

"*Reginald,*" a distinct voice said on the other side.

Making sure that I could still hear Nikita bouncing about in the kitchen singing at the top of her lungs, I opened the door slightly and saw the ogre standing there in jeans and a T-shirt. How he managed to hide arms that were that hairy from Nikita was beyond me. He had an urgent, angry face on and was not hiding his voice. "*Is Nikita alright?*" he asked around his tusks.

"Oh hi Reginald, this isn't the best time... I've been attacked by a shirime," I said and saw the recognition and, I'm pleased to say, the admiration.

"You are alive?" he asked, looking down at my still quivering flagpole.

"Apparently," I responded, holding the front door open so that he could see what lay slumped in the corner.

His eyes widened with such a fierce of hunger on his face that I stepped away, both hands rising defensively. "Reginald?"

The ogre took a breath and reined himself in with startling control. "The shirime are deadly," he said. "But they fear ogres..."

Every word dripped with a kind of pulsating hunger. I looked from him to the monster assassin and back to him again. "Why?"

"Their poison drives the libido of all men wild," he said. "As you can tell from you and from me."

I looked down at him and then took a very deliberate step back. "Reginald?" I said hesitantly.

"They fear us because they are of no danger to us. But we are a big danger to them."

This wasn't good, I thought. You could tell when ogres were in heat because they grew horns everywhere. I knew shirime. They fed off of humans. This one would have killed me and eaten me and then eaten Nikita. They had voracious appetites for human flesh and preferred more tender morsels. She was still unconscious and I wondered just how hard I had kicked her. She had left teeth marks in my shin from the kick to her crotch.

"Give her to me and I will get answers for you," Reginald promised.

"I'm not sure about that," I said.

"You need to know how she got through your barrier and why I am not able to," he said, reaching out and tapping on an invisible wall that went bakam bakam bakam with each knock. "And why she was sent here to kill you. I will find this out."

"How?" I asked.

He bared his teeth and I recognised the look in his eyes. It was the same one I had worn only a few minutes earlier.

The music in the kitchen stopped.

"You have to make a decision, Ambassador," Reginald said.

ELEVEN

"Hope you know what you're doing," Keith said, drawing the taxi to a stop in front of the gates. "I know these sorts of people don't take well to unannounced visitors."

I paid the fare and got out. The air had a clingy dampness to it, combined with a cruel, smarmy breeze. The trees on the opposite side of the wall loomed, the sky was blackened, and the clouds were a dark blue bruised colour with the slight tinge of pink around the edges. The air stank of dread.

I walked up to the gates, but as I neared they locked with a pertinent clamp. I stood in front of them, hands in my pockets, then took a deep breath and puffed it all out. Darkness hung like curtains from the sky, and had draped itself across the trees beyond the gate up to the point that they crowded around the driveway.

I was trying to control my temper.

"I don't see an invitation this time," a voice said from its hole. This statement was followed by the sound of something very large unfolding itself out of something small.

"I don't need an invitation," I said. "I'm angry."

"Well, you are definitely not getting past those gates then are you?" the bogeyman said, hauling his incredible tall frame out of the hole, resembling in all manners a gigantic skeleton draped in grey, elephantine skin with long strands of wispy hair hanging off its long hunched back and off its droopy, scowling face. Dark beady eyes glared down at me with an intense anticipation and a foul stench of rotting meat assaulted my nostrils. It looked made up of skin and bone, but skin can be thick and bones can be very hard. All that I could see were the number of joints this poor monster had.

The slender man was waiting at the door with a smile frozen on its face. But behind the smile was a different expression entirely.

"Madam Thankeron is not expecting you," he said.

"I really don't care this time," I said.

"Please, *please* let me go!" the bogeyman wept.

"She is not accepting any guests," the slender man said.

"Trust me," I said. "Today I am not a guest."

"I brought you up the drive and you said you would let me go!" the bogeyman reminded me frantically. "You're hurting me!"

I stared resolutely at the blank, featureless part of that face above that paralysed smile, and when the slender man bowed slightly and stepped out of the way of the door I nodded once and released the bogeyman. The monster faceplanted the driveway, scurried away from me, accidentally knocking aside a parked Jeep. It whirled to face me, apologised profusely and sprinted into the forest, uprooting a tree or two and tripping over its feet.

"You have hidden depths of cruelty to you, Ambassador," the slender man observed as I stalked past him.

As before, things moved around the house constantly, but with the difference that now they moved away from me, the shadows scurrying away as if I held a bright light.

"Is she in her room?" I asked, mounting the stairs.

"No," the slender man said, following close behind. "*She* is not in her chamber. *She* is busy conducting business."

At the top of the stairs I turned and thrust my arm out, my hand encircling the slender neck as easily as I would my wrist. "Where is she?"

The smile widened just a little, as if the creature was enjoying this, and for a second it creeped me out, like when you touch something slimy in a moment of haste and then want to wipe your hand frantically with an antiseptic wipe.

"All you had to do is ask," he crooned revoltingly. "She is in her study, of course. I will be happy to guide you there."

I released the monster and stood aside, allowing him to take the lead.

As we walked I could feel and hear and occasionally see glimpses of the many creatures still patrolling the house. They clearly didn't know what to make of me. I was angry enough that I would have rejoiced at having to fight them all and would have died laughing.

71

We came to a single wooden door and the slender man held it open for me. Beyond in a large wooden chamber with a tall volute ceiling like those found in churches, with a roaring bonfire the size of a house, knelt Madam Thankeron.

Shadows danced frantically around her and as I stepped through and the slender man closed the door behind me.

There was movement on either side and I realised how large the room was, and that in here with me were her two beasts of dogs.

Madam Thankeron sat with her back to me, and assembled in front of her was an assortment of clay pots and jugs, each of them depicting some sort of feature, be it a face, a body or an arm. She poured water from one jug to another in a ritual that I did not understand, but could feel the power emanating off of it. Like the concussive wave that you can feel but cannot see, the power that rippled off these jugs and this passing of the water hit me hard enough to make my clothes tug on me.

Her two dogs kept to the shadows, unsure of what to do, but I could see them – great, fierce, gigantic beasts getting ready to attack at a single command from their master.

On top of the smell of these hounds, I could smell the herbs burning in the fire. The smoke was being blown out in ripples, thrust by the pouring of the water.

I reached under my jacket and withdrew the iklwa. "I need to speak with you," I said.

"How very formal for a man who intrudes with a weapon," she responded, without any surprise about my presence.

"I don't know who I can trust," I said. "So I have returned to my favourite tools."

"The iklwa is your favoured weapon?" she enquired, genuinely interested.

I didn't answer her. I wasn't going to be sidetracked. "Who was the man who gave me the invitation to your party the other night and who put a protection spell on my home the night later?"

"You know I cannot give you his name," she said. "Old Rules and all that."

"So you know him?"

72

"Of course," she said, still pouring the water from one jug to another. She would then put down the empty jug, select a fresh jug from another section of the collection, bring it near and pour the water from the other jug into that one. "But he is not an employee. I suppose he works for the same embassy that you do."

"Does he want me dead?"

"I can think of nothing he would stand to gain from your death," she said, still pouring. I realised I wasn't holding her full attention, and this bugged me.

"What do you gain from wanting me dead?"

"Absolutely nothing," she responded. "Can you enlighten me as to why you're asking me these questions?"

"I've been attacked at my house by two different assassins over the last two days."

"You did not decide to move after the first attack?"

"Your friend put a protective spell on the house between them," I said. "And I will not run from my home. I like it there."

"Maybe the spell was faulty?" she suggested, speaking around the pouring noise of the water flowing from one vessel to another. "Or broken?"

"It worked on an ogre," I said. "Who explained that a protective spell is merely a door."

"Yes, and that to get through it you must possess a key," she finished off neatly. "You believe that I gave these two assassins a key to your apartment with the intention of having you killed?"

"No," I corrected, "I am suggested you sent the first assassin to kill me and when he failed you then asked your friend to put up the spell to stop my housemate's new boyfriend from helping me fight off the second assassin, who you gave a key to. In all of the Otherwise I can only think of one person who could afford a Needleman and a shirime demon in the same week."

"It is an interesting theory," she said, looking over her collection of jugs, her hand hovering over them, her fingers dancing through the air as if playing a chord on some hidden strings. "Intriguing, no doubt. But you assume that I would have something to gain from your death… don't forget I am still waiting for you to do me a favour."

"This is my problem, you see," I said. "You don't have anything to gain from killing me, but I know that it was you, Madam Thankeron, who sent the assassins after me."

"Oh?"

"My ogre friend had a word with the shirime."

Madam Thankeron's red tattooed hand hesitated over a jug abruptly. "Is she alive?"

"I don't think she'd want to be," I said.

Her hand swung right and selected a jug, seemingly at random, and poured water into it. I was buffeted by more energy as I made a circle around her, standing next to the hearth that held the gigantic fire. Its warmth was almost unbearable.

"You let the ogre… have a word?" she asked. "I am astonished."

"She tried to kill me," I pointed out. "The ogre had a way of getting the answers from her."

"Did you watch him do it?" she asked innocently, casting her eyes up to mine.

I shook my head. "I had no need to… she said that you sent her, the lady with the red drawings, the first suitor of Adam."

She took in a breath but didn't cease in her administrations with the jugs and the water. I watched for a bit. The dogs were keen and following me but they had not attacked, and I knew that if I needed to fight it would be them first. They were otherwise still.

"I feel you have a question you want to ask me Donnie," she said.

"I have a couple. But you have to promise to answer them honestly, or else I will do something drastic."

She laughed. "Like what? You are in my chamber, in my house. My dogs are on hand and I have a houseful of nightmares waiting for my single word."

I pointed the iklwa blade at her. "Promise."

She shrugged. "Fine. I hate playing these kinds of games anyway. I promise to tell the truth."

"Why didn't you send a vampire to kill me? Or a hex? They would have been more proficient."

"As I said, I do not benefit from your death... yet... I had to send assassins that you could fight."

"So this was a test," I said. "The ogre was right?"

Madam Thankeron smirked. "Do you ever do your own thinking?"

I ignored the question. "Why were you testing me?"

"There is an assassin that sneaked into my house," Madam Thankeron said. "Who almost managed to put an end to my life's work. I needed to be able to test you to see if you would be fit for the challenge of finding this assassin and stopping him."

"What if I don't want to stop him?"

"Oh you will," she said with resigned self-assuredness, changing the water of a larger jug into several smaller ones that belonged in a set. "It is in your nature... you protect that which needs protecting. You have seen what is in that room, you know what your favour will mean, even if you refuse now and deny any feelings. When you're lying in bed, in your quiet moments you will reach the decision that what needs to be protected must be."

"Who do you think sent the assassin?"

"That... I honestly don't know," she said.

"Do you think the assassin somehow wants to stop me helping you?"

"Clearly."

"I mean before I do this favour."

"Do you mean will he stop if you do the favour?"

"Yes."

"Perhaps, it is definitely worth a try. But I have the suspicion that once the favour is done he may well be more incensed to try again. But if you don't do the favour and he succeeds then a great deal more will be lost."

I considered it for a long time, watching her change that water and eventually said, "Fine. But no more assassins at my house."

"Fair enough."

"Also stop the barman from contacting me. I don't trust him at the moment and I'm not wearing that suit he said I should wear."

"Your new threads are looking much branded," she observed.

"When do you want me to do this favour for you?"

She stopped her pouring and for the first time in the conversation gave me her undivided attention. She smiled a smile of sheer delight. "You agree?" she asked. "You will help me?"

"Yes," I said. "But it is as tactical as it is a favour. It is a means of drawing the assassin out."

Madam Thankeron nodded in understanding. "Of course. I will begin arrangements immediately. Can you come back here tomorrow night and do the deed?"

"Yes."

"Good," she said, getting up and coming over and embracing me. "Thank you Donnie," she said into my neck crook. "Thank you so much."

Taking her shoulders and holding her at arm's length, I looked into those liquid blue eyes and said, "I will need some help though."

"I imagine so," she said.

"No, I meant that I will need to bring in someone else," I said. "To watch my back."

"Who?"

TWELVE

Nikita couldn't hide her coy smile when Reginald walked into the shop and ducked to get under the door. Ogres, like cats, exist in both sides of the line at the same time. They're like shirts and pants, tucked into each other. In Aroma you saw what you wanted to. Those who were Otherwise saw an ogre and those who were human saw a very well-dressed and powerful looking human.

As a matter of interest, if a cat had strolled into Aroma some would have just seen a domesticated cat whereas the Otherwise probably would have fled out the back entrance. Reginald's human and ogre appearances, for all the differences they offered, were nothing in comparison to the transforming difference that a simple domestic cat could undergo.

Reginald answered her grin with his own beaming smile before it faded like breath on a mirror when he spotted me. Sitting in the corner talking on my phone, as he came in, I avoided Nikita's gaze, picked up my coffee and headed to the stairs, focused on the call.

Reginald joined me upstairs after a little while.

"Hello Ambassador," he said, in way of greeting.

"Hello," I said, looking at him closely.

"You have friends in Sweden?" he enquired, gesturing to my phone with a flick of a finger. "And you're fluent in Dutch?"

"One of my first assignments as Ambassador was to liaise with CERN when they created that portal."

Reginald whistled through his teeth. "That must have been interesting for you."

"It was an eye opener," I agreed. "So now they owe me a favour and I was just asking them to courier me a little present."

"I almost didn't come today," he said, seating himself and immediately playing with his cup, turning it around in the saucer with his giant hands. They were human hands, as such. I allowed my eyes to relax, to stop seeing what my mind wanted them to see. The hands didn't change shape, they didn't morph or transform, the camouflage that the ogre used was as much of its genetics and physical chemistry as the colouring of a chameleon. Instead what I saw were big human paws, the big callused mitts of a man accustomed to working with his hands. Hairy forearms knitted with pale scars. That's what my eyes saw – but what I perceived were that they were actually gigantic paws capable of doing the same damage to my body that I could do with a newly hatched chick.

"I had no doubt that you would," I said. "You said you would."

"I am ashamed of what I did last night," he said to me, avoiding my gaze.

"You got the answers from the demon as I needed," I said, levelly. "I'm really not in the position to question your methods."

That's what I said, but there was a big part of me that didn't want to be within touching distance of him. That he harboured regret was little consolation for what he had done. Memories of that shirime clawing at the floor as he dragged her out of the apartment by an ankle would stay with me for a long time. I wouldn't remember her as a demon that had tried to eat me, but rather as a red headed girl crying in genuine terror. I hadn't watched what had happened but I heard it from my window. It does not take an imaginative mind to work out what's happening by the way someone screams. There is a sound that a body makes when it is injured in such a way that steals the breath away from even a scream.

"Nevertheless," he said resolutely, "I have worked very hard to integrate myself into this world, and if I'm honest I did not want you to see me like that."

"I have no opinion."

"You are Nikita's housemate," he said. "Of course you do."

"I am also the Ambassador," I added, although unnecessarily.

"Yes, but not a spectacularly good one," he pointed out, then apologised. "Forgive me, I didn't mean to be rude. That was uncalled for."

I waved it off. "I am gifted with overconfidence," I said. "It's a good substitute for education and talent. I just pretend to know

78

what I'm doing and wait for everything to fall into place. It seems to have worked so far."

"Well," he said, sipping his coffee, during which for a brief second I thought I spied his tusks. "You have survived two assassin attacks. So you must have some talent. Is it true what the whispers say about you?"

Ah, the whispers. Humans have social media and texting, but the Otherwise and Late have the whispers that float like mists and whisper secrets and gossip, warnings and news.

"I don't know what they say so I can't comment..."

"They say that the Ambassador is a trained assassin."

I expected what happened next. I had tested Miss Beebe in a similar fashion and if someone says to me that they were a master at origami the first thing I would do is hand them a napkin and ask them to prove it.

While in transit the ogre's arm seemed to quadruple in size, but moved with twice the speed of the arm of a world-champion level boxer. I only moved my head a fraction to the right to avoid the punch while my right hand, armed as it was, extended up and stopped as it pressed against the hard rope-knot of his Adam's apple. Our eye contact never broke.

He cleared his throat awkwardly and lowered his arm. His aim had been precise, and his forearm had been so close I could smell the fabric of his suit jacket sleeve.

I lowered my weapon and placed it back onto the coffee saucer. The ogre cocked an eyebrow at the teaspoon.

"Well?" I asked.

"My question is answered," he said.

"Tell me how?" I asked. I wanted to know if he was just bluffing.

"Many people have reflexes," he said. "Most people, both human and Otherwise, will be able to avoid an attack but they will jump out of the way."

I sipped my coffee, waiting for him to continue.

"You avoided it enough so that you would be able to trap it, while countering at the same time with the most applicable attack.

The difference is how casual and calm you were. Not very fast, just direct and thoughtless."

"Why does it interest you?" I asked.

"I want to know who her current protector is," he said.

"I am not her protector," I said. "She doesn't need one."

This was true. The fact of the matter was that if she had seen me fighting with the shirime the night before she probably would have only seen me fighting with a small redhead woman. If I see a bee it looks the size of a fly, but if you're highly allergic to bees, when you see them they are gigantic, evil and terrifying. We see things according to the danger they pose to us. Nikita saw Reginald as a human because, even with him as an ogre, she had no need to be afraid.

"Have you never asked why nobody has tried to awaken Nikita or her family to the truth of their power?"

"I don't pry," I said.

"Do you want to know?"

"I do now."

His eyes narrowed. The heavy brows made this a very significant expression. "You're a cunning one, Ambassador," he said. "You put on this persona of a bumbling idiot, but it's all a game of chess to you. You are like a hangman who lets the condemned tie their own knots."

"People tend to think that," I admitted. "Why hasn't anyone done it?"

"Let's just say that their revelation could have consequences and it is important that they remain ignorant for now. She and her family need to realise who they are when they are ready to do so. It is a natural development, a metamorphosis of purpose. Bring them into it too soon and it could be tragic."

"That isn't as much of an answer as you think it is," I pointed out. "Don't you know?"

"Nobody knows," he said. "Their bloodline is very old."

"Everyone's bloodline is very old," I reminded him. "We're all directly related to the first fish that crawled out of the ocean. What's special about theirs?"

He shrugged. "No idea. But you live with her, so tell me... do you want to see her angry?"

The thought actually made me shiver a little. "It's not my place to reveal anything to her anyway," I said. "But you're right. I've always known there was something special about her and I've lived with her longer than I've been Ambassador."

Reginald's lips pressed into a tight line and he waited for me to catch up with some big and obvious thing that was hanging in the air between us.

"Oh my God," I said.

"Yup," he replied with a quick nod. "Everyone knows that's why you got the shoebox."

Ever realised that there is a joke you've been sharing for years, not realising you were the punchline?

"I'm her distraction?"

"Everyone has talents, Ambassador," the ogre said. "You would be able to distract her from what she is by drawing the attention of the Late onto yourself. You are a walking calamity and that perplexes everyone and raises so many questions that it draws attention from her."

"But all the Late know who she is," I mumbled, as if this was actually to my credit somehow.

"All creatures can sense power and strength, but the distraction isn't to draw the Late's attention from her, it's to draw her attention away from the Late."

I put my elbows onto the table and my face in my hands. "I thought I was important."

"You *are* the Ambassador," Reginald said, taking a sip of his coffee. "But it isn't a position that is really needed. It is just convenient to have an impartial middle man."

"I'm basically a pair of jingling keys for an anxious baby," I said through my hands.

"You are also her protection," he pointed out.

"But she doesn't need protection," I said meekly.

"If she had been attacked by the shirime she would have protected herself. Unlike you, she doesn't know her strength or

81

how to control what she has. It would have been like using a stick of dynamite to kill a spider."

"Who are you?" I asked. "You're smarter than your average ogre."

"Good stock," Reginald said smugly. He put down his coffee and I saw that he had half a cup left. The coffee sign – it's a universal guy code, going across all species, that a conversation will continue as long as there is coffee in the cup.

"But who are you in the grand scheme of things?"

He smiled, and it was a charming grin for someone so big. "Don't get paranoid, Donnie," he said. "The whispers keep a lot of us informed, but I have an interest in this situation... my interest is in continuing to court Nikita. And I feared I crossed the line with you last night."

"I don't see it that way," I lied.

"May I continue to court Nikita in that case?" he said. "Assuming she maintains an interest in me."

"I have no say in that," I said, "But if you feel that you are in my debt I then do have a favour to ask of you."

"Okay?" he sounded dubious.

"I need to get Nikita out of Norwich for a while," I said.

"Why? Those two assassins were sent for you, not for her."

I winced. "There is more to this situation. From what you've said it's been dangerous keeping Nikita so close to it for this long. What are the chances you could take her away for a little while?"

"Where?"

"Anywhere, out of the city if possible, out of the country even."

"I have offices in the Canaries," he said, considering things. "I could take her for a holiday in the sun?"

"Offices?" I asked, completely thrown for a second.

"Yes, I own a vehicle rental company. Long and short term leases."

"International?" I asked.

He rolled his jaw at me, and I sat back in my chair. He said, "Yes, I am an ogre who owns an internationally recognised car rental company."

82

I took a breath and drank some more coffee. "The Canaries would be fine. Can you get her to go tonight?"

His jaw dropped. "*Get* her to go? Nikita?"

I scratched at my forehead, realising who I was talking about. "Ask her, figure out something really spectacular and beg her — if you have to, drug her, put her into a sack and drag her to the airport."

His jaw dropped a little further. "I hope it doesn't come to that," he said. "But I would like to treat her to something nice anyway. We have an agreement."

"Excellent," I said, standing and leaving before he finished his coffee.

THIRTEEN

Miss Beebe agreed to meet me at the flat and was punctual to the very minute. When she walked through the door without any trouble, I realised that it may have been a subconscious test I wanted answering. It meant she was human.

"Renovating?" she asked, looking at the intermingling repair and damage.

"I suppose," I said. "I am grateful that you could come."

She smiled. "I was curious to see the legendary Number 8 Tudor Hall."

"I would usually offer coffee, but I've already had too many cups this morning. Do you fancy something stronger?"

She checked her watch. "It is a bit early for me."

"Okay, how about some fruit juice?"

"That sounds lovely."

"Okay, I'll be right back. I need to go buy some fruit juice."

I walked at high speed to the local Tesco and bought a stash of fruit juice and some cheese and chutney sandwiches and rushed back, wondering why I had left a stranger in my house. When I returned she was sitting demurely on the edge of my hammock, paging through some of my books. I poured the juice, put the sandwiches on plates and asked what she had found out about our wayward assassin.

"Not much," she admitted. "It's all whispers and rumours, and I am totally out of reliable resources. I was able to find out more about him by what wasn't there."

"Like what?" I asked, already on my second glass of orange juice. After drinking so much caffeine I was trying to stop my hands from shaking.

"As you know, client records are kept secret," she said. "All hard copies, and paper files. No computers that can be hacked. So I couldn't find anything about who hired him or what his target is.

But an operative's communication is still maintained through deep encryption internet forums."

"I've never been able to hack them," I mentioned. The internet, as you know, is only the tip of a large and dark iceberg, representing only a meagre 7% of the actual internet. Nothing is ever lost online – it is simply buried. The surface internet is what is easy to find and navigate thanks to big search engines and websites and is highly media directed. The deep internet includes locked forums, invite only websites and, at the very, very bottom, coded communiques through old DOS systems.

Nowadays operatives, or assassins, got their information through flash drive drop points. You've probably walked past them without realising. A flash drive buried into the mortar of a wall with only the drive plug sticking out. These things are everywhere, tucked away and hidden in public places and only for those in the know.

When I was still operating I would sometimes spend my days wading through sewers, or climbing through abandoned buildings that for some reason remained empty and standing. A couple of the best hotel rooms in the world are drop zones.

Like cities, the world is built up in layers, and for the most part we're only aware of the layers we live in. The rest are just cellars or attics to us and we know nothing of the minds that creep around there.

"You need to know the right people to get in," she said. "If you hadn't gone freelance you would know it."

"I was expelled," I said bluntly. "There is a difference."

"Yes," she said. "Something you have in common with this chap."

"Really?"

"Yes, there was some reaction online about the assassin attack at Madam Thankeron's."

"It's what you would expect," I reasoned. "There are the Late who use the internet as much as any human."

"Yes," she said. "Where were you the night of the attempt?"

"Here," I said. "Redecorating with my own assassin. There are witnesses."

"What time were you attacked?" she asked.

"No idea... nine o'clock?"

"Given the discrepancies between our time and Otherwise time that leaves about a three hour window..."

"Yes, they're late," I agreed. "But the window could actually be quite longer than that. What is your point?"

"Were you the assassin?"

God, how many times was I going to hear something that would hit me like a punch to the guts? I ran my eyes quickly over her. She wasn't concealing any weapons, but that didn't matter. Suddenly the conversation had veered off in a direction I hadn't expected. I had been about to ask her to come help me at Madam Thankeron's to root out the assassin, but suddenly it seemed like I wasn't going to get the chance to ask.

"No," I said. "I'm not the assassin. Besides, I don't meet the description."

"You could fake the evidence we'd found so as to cover your tracks," she said. "You are very skilled."

"I think a lot of people overestimate me," I told her. Dammit, I had left that iklwa in my room.

She looked suddenly angry. "You know... part of my mission was to breed with you."

I was wrong, three times.

"Breed?" I croaked, my mouth and throat lined with cardboard.

"Yes," she said. "Genetically you're a good match and bloodlines are important for the school."

"That was your mission?"

"Of course. I do still work for the school."

"I guessed that," I said. "But why do they want my genes?"

"Only half of them," she pointed out. "You were expelled and they need the bloodlines to continue. It's about controlled breeding after all, isn't it?"

I was suddenly a five year old listening to his parents speak with other adults about a future he couldn't comprehend and realising that above him, just out of his conceptual reach, was a massive cloud of decisions, conspiracies, plans and tactics to control his life that he didn't know about. *While you sleep Donnie,* that voice said, *people are conspiring about you.*

"Um…" I realised I had lost the opportunity to ask my favour. I checked my watch. "I am busy tonight, but I've got a couple of hours to kill before I need to leave. Are you planning to kill me or shag me?"

"Well, I don't technically need to shag you to breed with you," she explained. "I guess it depends on you. Are you the assassin I'm hunting?"

Ice skating giraffes have more control of their destiny than I did of mine at that moment.

"I'm not playing this game, Vanessa," I said, standing and walking around the armchair to the kitchen so I could put some furniture between myself and her. I put the carton on the counter and scanned around the flat. Yet again I seemed to be playing catch up to everyone's plans, and there was an important rule every assassin learns at school. Always be a master of your surroundings.

I had left Miss Beebe in my flat. She could have accomplished anything in my short absence. My home could have been an Indiana Jones style den of booby traps and snares by now.

I leant back against the counter and stood as casually as I could, facing her. The assassin rose from the armchair and walked around it, facing me but standing around ten feet in distance.

"This is not a game," she said. "It makes perfect sense after all… you put on the masquerade of being a reckless playboy who is taking advantage of his token position, and meanwhile you're gaining information and details about your client. It's classic and very well done. Your instructors would be very proud. There are many members of the Otherwise parliament whose deaths would fetch a hefty reward. It was just a matter of you finding which one you could get closest to, and then finding a client willing to pay you enough money for it. Who was it?"

I blinked. Gobsmacked. "The Otherwise want me to find the assassin though, they sent two assassins to test whether I would be good enough to find him…"

Could you trust Madam Thankeron? I thought, *She's a Lilith. How do you know that they wanted to test you? What if they were genuine assassination attempts?*

"It wasn't me," I said. "I'm not the assassin. He's still out there."

"I don't believe you," she said. "But it doesn't matter. I don't have to tell anyone that I found the assassin responsible. We can do a deal."

"A deal?" The incredulity in my voice was thick.

"Yes, my mission was twofold. To breed with you and to find the assassin. Breed with me and I'll leave."

This couldn't be happening.

"I don't want to be a father," I said.

"Pfft," she snorted. "Who said anything about *you* being a father? You're donating your seed, not raising a child. You will never meet it."

She didn't need to set any traps, I thought. I had already fallen for hers.

"I am not going to breed with you," I said. "You'll have to cut it out of me."

"Technically I don't need you to be alive," she said. "Although it is better if it's natural. Works better that way, you see."

"No," I said.

A grin tickled the corner of her mouth.

The opening gambit of her attack was a slap to my face, which I saw coming and let happen because I wanted to judge her commitment. This was an error. With my ears ringing and one side of my face on fire we grappled for a moment, her hands trying to find purchase around my neck and over my shoulders in an attempt to get me to the ground and wrestle – but this was a ruse, meaning to distract my attention to what our arms were doing while she jumped fully into the air in a specific frontal motion with her knee targeted to my groin.

Prepared for this I moved forward, making use of my height and grabbed her leg between my thighs. Less to do with the pinching strength of my inner legs and more to do with the surface traction of my trousers I captured her limb, stepped in towards her so that my leading leg was between her legs and applied some well-timed hip-force that threw her off balance. I had her shoulders in my hands by this time, and utilising her inertia I pushed with my right hand, pulled with my left and shoved her away.

My God she recovered fast. She instantly re-engaged and we entered into a proper combative engagement.

This is not like you see in the films. Real fighting isn't about well timed, gracious choreography and delicate attacks. An opponent will never stand open for you to attack them. Instead, real fighting is all about gaining an advantage in a storm of punches and kicks.

My advantage was my size and strength. Hers was that she really, *really* wanted to hurt me.

It was a stampede of hands and feet, knees and elbows. She would latch onto anything I gave her and pummel it with whatever weapon she had available. In movies people take the most incredible hits – face punches that don't break noses or knock out teeth but are still able to take them off their feet, or punches to the ribs that should kill but barely wind. I guarded myself like a boxer, fists up by my temples, forearms shielding my face, tucked down so that my elbows could field her blows. I saw openings, many, many openings but I couldn't bring myself to hit her because I didn't want to hurt her.

"Fight me dammit!" she shrieked, raining big windmilling blows against my head in an attempt to make me attack the openings that such big-bazooka strikes created.

In response I put a hand flat on her chest bone and pushed her away with a thrust of my arm. She fell into the armchair, planted her feet and threw a low muay-thai roundhouse kick that I fielded with my own leg, which was then cocked for a low donkey kick. The flat of my shoe hit her at waist height, about four inches under the belly button. She folded as her pelvis was kicked backwards and mechanically she couldn't help the surprised hiccup sound that came out her throat.

I engaged with her this time, not intending to hurt but intending to neutralise.

I opened with several straight punches, then a couple of easily blocked elbows. I went for muscle seams, using the wing chun punches with a loose wrist and late clench to strike at the weakest part of the arms and legs – the kind of punches that can bruise a muscle down to the bone and leave the user of that muscle with what we used to call a dead arm.

Make an injury and continue attacking it.

It meant that my defences became offensive. She would throw a kick and instead of blocking or dodging it as if it were a fiery blade I'd hook a fist into the muscular cushion just above the knee. If she threw a punch I'd tiger pinch the sinews under the arm. This slowed down each of her attacks and she had to change her strategy to accommodate.

Disengaging with me she stepped backwards, shaking her arms, and leant on the wooden bow of my hammock stand for a moment, her belly inflating with each breath. I straightened up, revisiting the position that I did not want to fight her and that this was pointless. My body stung and ached in a hundred different places, but I kept my shoulders back and my chin high.

When you feel small look big, when you're big look small.

"You're quite the fighter," she heaved.

"So are you," I replied as evenly as I could. "You don't have to pretend you're tired though. I won't be embarrassed."

She shrugged and stood straight, any sign of her exhaustion slipping away like water. *Dammit.*

"Do we have to fight?" I asked.

"Not at all," she said with a meaningful grin. "There are a number of things I'd rather be doing."

I felt resolute.

She took a big breath, as if exasperated, and sat down on the carpet. She had become a child sitting down on the floor and promising a tantrum, and this lasted until she started to pull off her boots.

"What are you doing?" I asked.

"Not fighting," she said, placing the boots delicately together out of the way and adding, "They are genuine leather."

Unbuckling her belt, she pulled it from her jeans. She rolled it up and put it into her boot, then unbuttoned the front of her denims. Her eyes locked on mine as she slipped her thumbs into the seams of her trousers and wriggled out of them.

"Vanessa," I cautioned, backing up. "Don't."

Her legs were long and athletic, patches of red up and down the otherwise silky smooth pale limbs, which promised to turn into horrible brown-grey bruises, but they were the kind of legs that would look good anyway. She was wearing a back thong – I say thong because 'decorative shoe lace' is the only other description.

She slung the jeans away, and I was reminded of all those times I had reason to buy a bottle of rum, open it and throw the cap away because I had no intention of leaving anything in the bottle. Miss Beebe had no intention of putting those denims back on.

For a second she sat provocatively, leaning back against my pile of books with her legs spread, her blouse tight against her breasts and straining the buttons. My eyes found their way to where that wonderfully skimpy thong failed to hide that she was a fan of the Hollywood. She ran her fingers over her legs, her finger tips indenting the skin of her thighs like the surface of a silk sheet.

"Vanessa," I said, dry-mouthed. "Get dressed."

As if mishearing me, she moved her hands up her body, briefly running them through where her fringe was covering her face, before bringing them down her throat to the buttons that she started to undo. Each one sprang open with glee.

I had to remain still. If I moved, any gesture would have given away my unease and rewarded her with a weakness. I wanted to fiddle with my hands, I wanted to adjust my own clothing where it had been pulled out of place. I was uncomfortable. My boxers had ridden up, my face was itchy with sweat, but any sort of movement would have given me away.

Of the seven buttons holding her cleavage in place, she unbuttoned three at the top and three at the bottom. There was no denying the woman was attractive. Abdominal muscles reached from the half-moon undersides of her breasts down to the flat panel of flesh leading into that tiny thong, and cords of muscle beckoned seductively at the corners of her hips.

That final button teased.

"If you really want me to get dressed, you'll have to do it yourself," she crooned.

In hindsight, there were many ways that I should have approached this. I could have called someone, anyone, from a wide selection of people, ranging from friends to family, to come to the flat and help me. I could have opened the window and screamed that there was a woman undressing herself in my apartment, and surely someone would have come. When you're thinking of these things after the event it does really seem quite simple and straightforward, but I wasn't thinking about any of that then. I was thinking that I had just been fighting, my heart was drumming in my ears and I had a cocktail of adrenaline and testosterone pumping through my system – and a very attractive woman had just started playing with herself in my living room.

"I'll warn you," she said, "I do tend to make a mess..."

Her abdomen was smooth and hairless and so moistened with sweat that, while her fingers may have accidentally slipped beneath the flimsy front of the thong as if by accident, they were happy to remain where they ended up. Her middle finger was moving rhythmically between the capping guards of her other fingers.

I could hear the succulent wet sounds.

"It is time to go," I squeaked.

"You are welcome to make me leave," she said.

"I will," I said.

"Go on then."

"Don't make me."

"I plan to."

She winked.

"I'll leave," I threatened.

"Go on then," she said, nodding to the door before her face blanked and her eyes closed, her sigh signalling she was becoming overcome with satisfaction. "If you want to leave you can. I'll make myself at home and wait for you to return."

"This isn't fair," I said.

"No," she agreed, "I don't think it is."

Her free hand went up and cupped her breast before unbuttoning the button, which gave way with a pop. Her breasts sprang out – light pink nipples against pale skin. My mouth went from dry to being filled with water. She teased a nipple and with her hand that was occupied between her legs she added another finger to the delving motion and bit her bottom lip.

This had gone far enough, I decided. You'll be pleased to know that I took the moral high ground and was not going to be forced into a situation. I took her by the arm and hauled her to her feet, planning to deposit her outside my flat and lock the door!

FOURTEEN

But would you believe it? She attacked me!

And before I knew it I was lying flat on my back with my clothes stripped off! For some reason, my socks managed to survive this devious attack but everything else was taken from me and, with renewed vigour and incredulous strength, she had pinned me to the ground. Holding my wrists behind my head with her hands while straddling my stomach, she rhythmically moistened my abs while bumping her buttocks against the quivering tip of my enraged cock.

Her hot breath against the side of my neck, she nuzzled her face against my flesh, nipping the skin there with deceptive reserve, then drew her cheek up against mine until our lips met and we kissed – by which I mean she kissed me. Her lips crushed mine and her tongue invaded my mouth, searching out my tongue, teasing it before withdrawing.

All the while I could feel drips of moisture cascading down my flanks as she churned herself against me, her buttocks beating out a rhythm against my bell-end.

She drew back and looked me in the eyes and gave a wicked, dimpled smile. "You see? This is better."

I didn't respond, but tried to get my arms free. She wasn't letting me. Her grip had become vice-like and supported by a strength that had been thoroughly nailed down. Her eyelids fluttered and her lips curled back away from her teeth as she rubbed herself against me and teased my penis. She adjusted her grip on my wrists so that she held both of mine in one hand and reached behind her and stroked my shaft up and down, grazing lightly with her fingertips before encircling it with her hands. Her eyes widened and she bit her bottom lip with glee, giving me a devilish expression.

"You *are* playing my game now, aren't you?"

"No," I said, struggling against the strength of her one hand. "I am still fighting you and I will continue fighting..."

She had arched her hips back and brought them down upon me so that her lips sucked on either side of my shaft, and she slid back the full length of my member until my head popped out from between us. She looked at me questioningly. "You were saying?"

"...you," I managed.

She continued to slide up and down me, teasing me with her incredibly wet, silken touch. While one hand held both my wrists, her other pressed against my chest to steady herself. It seemed that she was trying to control herself as much as me and that this was as much an opportunity to tease herself.

She let her breasts go and her hard pink nipples grazed my face, and I drew one of them into my mouth and gave it a nip.

"That's not exactly fighting me," she said, squirming against me so that my cock head was engulfed in her fiery heat.

"I'm luring you into a false sense of security," I growled, just as my traitorous hips gave a buck.

"Oh yes," she said, adjusting herself. "I can tell that."

She reached between her legs and chuckled. "I am so wet, I'm going to leave a puddle!"

In a swift movement she clambered up, so that she pinned my arms with her knees and her genitals hovered inches above my face. I gazed up and couldn't help the reaction that I had as my cock suddenly throbbed so hard it almost buzzed. Her vagina was spectacularly packaged, the folds of flesh opening up in perfect harmony like a flower with a budded head of a clit the same size as her nipples at the top. Wet and pink, it looked sweeter than candy and I looked up past it, past her body to where she was looking down at me over her breasts.

When I did not immediately respond she ran her fingers through my hair, took hold of my head and physically hauled my face into her expecting wetness. It was the kind of sexual aggression that negates foreplay and I was helpless but to respond.

I focused all my attention on her clit, using the middle of my tongue to stimulate the underside of it and licking with long drawn strokes. I listened to her moans, the physical cues of how her body ground against my head, how her hands guided me to where she needed me to go.

I struggled to breathe, having to take gulps of air when her body moved away, because it was like she was trying to smother me with her crotch and, as her arousal peaked, it was close to being waterboarded by government spies. When she came it was in a gush that flooded my mouth and poured over my face and her thighs clamped around the sides of my head so powerfully that for a second I forgot where I was entirely, locked in a helmet-darkness between her legs.

Her body quivered, her thighs vibrating on the sides of my head and she let out a long list of expletives and curses as if she wanted to make the walls blush.

Clamped where I was I continued to lap at her hard nub of a clitoris and her hands left my head. I felt her knuckles brush against my throat as she sought out her anus and rimmed herself with her finger tips.

However, at the last orgasm she sprung off me like a cat getting a fright and my head cracked against the floor.

She stood over me, turned around and planted her feet carefully, then lowered herself down on me so that she could use her mouth on me while I continued with my lascivious lapping.

Her mouth was so hot and expectantly welcoming that I had almost triggered, and to stop myself I buried my tongue into her moist opening, my nose pressing against the flesh between her holes, my eyes falling upon her beautifully cute, almost prettily puckered arse. The forceful nature of my tongue made her gasp, which helped, and when she went back to sucking me again and using her balled fists to stroke my cock from the root of my shaft up and over the tip as if polishing it, I dipped my thumb inside her and then, with almost reckless abandon, pressed the wet digit hard into her arse.

Some girls buck at this, some girls swear and others laugh – she yipped and pushed back until my thumb slid up to the knuckle inside her.

At least she's definitely not a shirime, I thought, as I resumed my administrations to her nethers.

"Oh my God you're good at that!" she breathed, clawing her fingernails down the length of my legs to grasp hold of my testicles. She rolled them, gently but with great enthusiasm, while she took my full length into her mouth, her torso convulsing as she did.

She came again, hard and wet, soaking my throat and chin, crying out in a kind of panic and trying to escape, scampering off me, her hands flying to her crotch, where she vigorously rubbed at herself while swearing in the most colourfully foul language. On her front, her firm, squatter's ass thrust up in the air so invitingly, I was on her in an instant. Crushing her flat onto the carpet with my full weight, she shrieked in angry surprise and struggled against me, trying to push herself up against my weight, but I wrapped my left arm around her throat, using my shoulder to press her neck into the crook of my arm, immobilising her neck while with the other hand I forced it under her, so that I took the skin off my knuckles against the carpet until I found the cascade of wetness between her legs and her hard, bulging clitoris.

Letting it slip between my fingertips I rubbed at it and held her in place while she squirmed under me, my hard cock sliding between her buttocks, my penis head grazing against her sensitive holes and teasing her.

Her profanity had become just guttural growls and shrieks until her body was stiffening against me and a wet explosion splashed between my fingers as she sunk her teeth deep into my forearm.

In turn I bit her earlobe, adjusted my hips until I found a willing opening then, using the leverage of the headlock, I pulled on her body at the same time as thrusting in with all the strength I could muster.

Her entire body went rigid with what was pure surprise — she arched her back against me and gave an airless, dry gasp as if the breath had been taken away from her.

I was suddenly reminded of the noise the shirime had made.

Miss Beebe didn't move for ages, her muscles remained taut and tight, and for a terrifying moment I thought she was going to drop dead.

She exhaled and relaxed, drawing her hands together and putting her face into them and slowly, gently at first, moving her buttock against me in slight circulating motions.

"I didn't expect that," she whispered, sniffing loudly.

Still inside her to my root I asked her, "Did you expect me to go gently?"

"No," she wheezed. "Still... it was unexpected."

"I went in the wrong hole," I observed, looking down between us. Gods, the line of back was sexy.

"No, you didn't," she assured me, in a husky voice. "You would have known, I would have died!"

"This isn't the hole I was aiming for," I said.

Her insides clenched and massaged my circumference, kneading my cock head and my crown — hot, wet and tight — while her movements, how she gyrated against me and moved against me, were trained. She had received schooling, and it was like she had been schooled on exactly how to satisfy me. This was a dangerous game I was playing. I had to put a stop to it, and the beast mentality was shouldered out of the way for a brief second as my rational mind rose to the surface of the mire. *Get out, nothing good will come of this.*

I started to pull out.

Her fingertips grabbed hold of my scrotum, pulling into the skin with her nails. Not painfully, but securely. She could have said, "Mine."

Fuck it, I thought.

I unravelled my arm from around her neck, grabbed hold of her shoulders, my fingers crushing my palms against her trapezius, and in the moment she took a breath as she anticipated what was coming.

Jackhammers have shattered concrete with more tenderness. There are railroad spikes that have entered the ground more gently than I entered her. This wasn't about sex, this wasn't about orgasm

– this was about me fucking this woman so hard that she wouldn't be able to sit right for days. Each thrust was aimed for the top of her head, every hump intended to split her in half, and every collision of our bodies intended to pound her pelvis into dust. I was going to fuck her so hard that she would need to be in traction, her immediate destiny was a full body cast. I was a god, I was a hero!

Grunting through gritted teeth on each of my thrusts, she clawed at the carpet, reaching back to put a hand against my abdomen in an attempt to slow me. I slapped her hand away, grabbed her waist and went harder.

The blunt, rounded knob of my penis crashed into her cervix with each thrust, her buttocks rippled with every impact of my pelvis against her. The muscles in her arms and legs shook with each stroke.

"You're fucking killing me!" she screamed.

"Fucking die happy then!" I replied, drawing back my hand and landing it hard against her buttock with a spread-fingered slap that echoed around the flat and left my ears ringing.

This was as far from love-making as could be. This was what fire is to art, a hammer is to a clay sculpture. Not about pleasure, but about power. This was hatred and anger, rage, fire and dominance. This was the kind of sex that terrifies and addicts.

I felt myself getting close to triggering and the world became empty, void, and we were the only living things. Joined together in our rage and anger.

I triggered.

It wasn't a localised orgasm. It was a surge of torturous pleasure that was dragged from every cell of my body, from my fingers, toes and scalp. I was hollowed out, everything of me drawn into a tight ball in my lower belly that for a second tightened. It was an instant that felt like it lasted forever for the silence it brought before it erupted in a spewing geyser deep inside her.

I was still thrusting, giving myself to wayward abandonment, pounding as I came again and again in long spewing ribbons inside her until the sound of our pounding changed.

It wouldn't end.

I forgot my name, I forgot where I was. It overtook mere pleasure as the orgasm sought to turn me inside out.

Even afterwards I continued pounding, every thrust scouring the sensitive length of my penis but I kept going, grunting and cursing and sweating until I collapsed onto her with exhaustion.

She was whimpering and she had torn through my carpet with her fingertips. From the hollowed out husk that I had become, anger began to rise (not because of the carpet), and she tensed.

"Are you going to kill me?" she asked quietly.

"Maybe not," I said, pushing myself up and away from her.

I had a timely shower, shaved and dressed in the suit. When I returned, she had dressed herself and was standing defensively near the counter. Conveniently, one of the knives Nikita used to cut meat had magically appeared on the counter. She looked apprehensive. Had she really never considered that I could have killed her afterwards? Had the thought really not occurred to her until after the event? She looked me up and down, deciding if I was dressed like a man about to commit murder.

"I need a favour," I said.

"You serious?" she asked.

"Yes," I said. "Now."

FIFTEEN

Pulling up the handbrake and turning off the ignition, Keith stared at us in the rear-view mirror, his eyes focusing longer on Miss Beebe.

"Are you sure about this?" he asked me, his fingers drumming out a nervous beat on the steering wheel.

I tossed some extra notes into the passenger seat and said, "Pretty sure."

Still uncertain, the driver mumbled something to himself, twisted the key and disengaged the handbrake. He pulled away from the curb sharply so that the taxi made a space in the flow of the traffic rather than joining it.

I leant back into the seat and said to Miss Beebe, "Are you okay?"

"You don't have to be soothing just because you shagged me half to death," she snapped (the taxi driver's head moved a fraction to the side).

"I hope it's what you really wanted," I said.

"Well we will see won't we?" she said. "The deal was that you would get me pregnant, I don't know if you've done the deed yet. So I'm afraid you're stuck with me. And in the meantime I will keep your secret."

"I am not the assassin you're looking for," I said.

"These *are* the assassins you're looking for," the taxi driver said, then slunk shamefully into his seat.

"You keep saying," she said to me. "But I don't think you can prove it."

"Actually, that is why I'm taking you to Madam Thankeron's." I said.

She glared at me. "What?"

People do that. We all get so worked up in our own self-involvement that we make assumptions about what is actually happening without just paying attention.

"Where did you think we were going?" I asked.

"I hadn't given it any thought," she admitted. "I'm feeling a little addle-brained."

I winked. "You're welcome."

On the journey up the hill I received a text from Nikita.

"*I'VE JUST BEEN KIDNAPPED BY REGINALD AND AM ON A PLANE TO THE CANARIES. YOU AND ME ARE GOING TO HAVE A WORD WHEN I GET BACK – IN TWO WEEKS (DID YOU KNOW YOU'RE ALLOWED TO USE YOUR MOBILE PHONE IN IN FIRST CLASS?) R says hi. XX*"

"Why are you taking me to Madam Thankeron's house?" Miss Beebe asked.

"You wanted to know what the favour was that I agreed to help her with."

"I did," she said. "Is that what you're going to show me?"

"It is something you're going to have to see for yourself," I explained. "And it'll show why I am not the assassin that you're looking for. I also think it's going to help you find the assassin though."

"This sounds interesting," she said. "Can you explain why?"

"The assassin didn't miss his target when he first broke into Madam Thankeron's mansion," I explained, peering out the window at the period houses as they trailed past. "He found the target but could not complete his contract."

"Can you tell me who the contract was at least?" she asked.

"I could," I said, "I really could, but it would be pointless. You're going to have to trust me on this one."

Keith, the taxi driver, took several turns, passing buildings, houses, shops, passing under bridges and driving us past large graveyards. Gradually the sky became dimmer as time was squeezed by in these folded spaces.

"Why are you carrying that iklwa?"

"I feel safer with it."

"Whose is it?"

102

I shrugged. "I thought it was Nikita's but I'm not sure now. I think it has something to do with protection from the embassy."

"You have no idea do you?"

"None," I admitted. "I didn't ask Nikita about it so maybe I've just stolen a family heirloom."

"May I?" she asked, holding out a hand with her other hand under her forearm. It would have seemed a strange gesture to anyone who had not grown up in KwaZulu-Natal during the 17th Century.

I handed it over and she inspected the weapon, passing her sure fingers over the surface of it, delicately touching the sharp edges of the spearhead. "This has seen blood," she observed.

"I know. Human and Otherwise."

"Is your housemate South African?" she asked.

"Not that I know of," I said. "What do you know about the Impi?"

"Shaka Zulu was an impressive leader and he revolutionised their weapons," she said, handing the weapon back. "You mentioned the embassy... why?"

"A messenger, or an operative... I think I prefer *operative* of theirs said that he had arranged protection. But this was in between them sending two assassins to try and kill me. I assumed he was talking about this suit, but it could just as easily have been this weapon. I'm not sure."

"Has your suit protected you?"

"I haven't been attacked in it yet."

"Did you consider asking?"

"Not for a second," I answered. "Either way I'm either right or I'm wrong."

"Yes, but if you're wrong..."

"I'll think of something."

She gave it back to me and my fingers curled around the handle possessively. I liked the weapon – was that a wrong reason to have it near?

The answer was yes, and both I and the assassin sitting next to me knew this. You couldn't have a preference for any weapon. You used a weapon for what it was intended and discarded it after. A simple but effective lesson, when at school we were taught the traditional uses of many weapons and then, during our exams, were given only everyday objects that we were made to use in combat. That way you soon realised how efficient a weapon a spade can be.

But it made me feel confident and I needed confidence, especially with what I was going to do.

We entered into a new portion of the city, where the gothic architecture rose in blocky, sharp edges on all sides like ravine walls. Gargoyles, condemning statues and twisted crucifixes glared down at us with judgement.

"Where are we?" Miss Beebe asked.

"Norwich City," Keith said from the front.

"I've never seen this," she said pointing up at the buildings. "Where are we?"

Keith and I shared a moment in the rearview mirror. He decided to take the lead. "Your city is a big one, miss," he explained, as he guided the car past darkened figures on horseback. The twilight sky was a slender grey rail above us now, and in the shadows of the doorways and buildings on either side things moved. "Very big," he continued. "But the space it can occupy on the map is much smaller, so they did the same thing you do when you want to a fit a coat into a small travel bag. You just fold it. With me?"

"I understand the theory," she said curtly. "I'm not a fool."

"Then you understand that this is just a part of the city that you haven't been to yet. Did you think you'd seen all that this city has to offer?"

She stared meekly out of the window.

I had not been to this part of the city either. "Keith, why have we come this way?"

"There was a road block on the other route," he said. "Not an official one of course, but a barrier nonetheless. They had some pretty dangerous looking people there if you know what I mean, and they were checking road users. I figured you probably wanted to avoid all that."

"You know who set it up?"

"I only hear what I hear," the taxi driver said happily.

104

I held up some more notes.

"What I've heard is that someone doesn't want you to do the favour for Madam Thankeron," he said.

I put the money back into my wallet. Keith rallied. "Has anyone given you something?" he asked.

I put the wallet back into my jacket.

"And I don't mean something useful, something recent that has proven to be totally useless and perhaps that you have forgotten about until now."

I took out my wallet again and opened it. Inside was a white business card, so I held it up so Keith could see it. He held his hand back over his shoulder. "Gimme," he said.

I handed it to him and, without taking his eyes off the road, Keith massaged the card between his thumb and forefinger, then pushed a button on the door panel and wound down his window. A cold air that smelt of smoke rushed in from the gap and he slipped he card out and let it go. The white strip of cardboard went fluttering past my window in a blur and became a twisting shape behind us.

"*Never* trust a slender man," Keith said in a hard voice. He wound up the window and the silence that followed was heavy. Even Miss Beebe seemed to have crept into her seat. The driver continued – "Never, ever, ever *ever* trust a goddamn slender man!" He slammed his palm against the steering wheel. "Ever!"

"I don't understand what's happening." Miss Beebe said.

Ignoring her, Keith asked me, "Do you have a barrier up at your home?"

"Yes," I said.

"Has it been invaded recently?"

"What have you heard?" I asked.

"That you were attacked by a Needleman and then by an eyeball-ass. When you didn't flee the country after the Needleman, I thought you were brave but then I heard that you gave the shirime to an ogre and thought you were just twisted. That's what I heard."

"Accurate," I said. "Why is the card important?"

"Trust," the driver said. "*Trust.* You took his card which means you *gave* him your trust."

"Excuse me," Miss Beebe said sharply, trying to use her assassin voice on the driver. He gave me a look again, as if to ask *is she for real?*

Miss Beebe asked, "What is a slender man?"

Keith, his ears red with frustration, growled. "A slender man gains the trust of its victims and then it slowly orchestrates their deaths. You've seen the memes online?"

She thought for a second. "The tall guy, featureless face?"

"Usually in a black suit," the driver confirmed. "Yes. They feed off children and other trusting fools," his eyes scathed my face through the rearview mirror. "Then slowly manipulate them into suicide."

"Seems awfully complicated," Miss Beebe pointed out.

"Norwich is Purgatory," Keith said. "There is more to the river that runs through it than you think. Suicides fetch a higher exchange with the boatman. Especially young suicides. The slender man deals in childhood suicides. In terrifying and tormenting the young until they take their own lives at which point their souls are taken by Chiron and these monsters make their cash. By taking his card, this trusting dope officially gave him his trust. Letting him in."

"Madam Thankeron said those assassins had been sent to test me," I argued.

"The slender man has been around longer than Lilith," the driver said. "They were some of the first manservants of death... who do you think controls who?"

Keith drew us up along the gates of Madam Thankeron's house. Turning around to face us, he said, "I will be on hand should you need me. Just give me a call." He looked at Miss Beebe. "I would suggest you let me take you home, Miss. You don't belong here."

"I'll stay," she said resolutely, opening the door and getting out.

"You're a fool," the driver said to me. "But I hope you're a lucky one."

I nodded and asked, "Do you like the water Keith?"

He let a moment, an all-important beat, pass – then, with a glint in his eye, replied, "I have a very thorough license."

I got out and he drove off. We both stared up at the looming gates and the epic black forest behind it.

"Doesn't look like anyone is home," Miss Beebe pointed out.

I walked up to the hole beside it. "Are you in there, Billy?"

A sullen voice echoed up from deep inside the hole. "Go away!" it whined. "I saw you coming and you're not going to hurt me again!"

The gate unlocked itself and I pulled it open for Miss Beebe, who was rubbing her arms. "Whatever that voice was, it's given me the heebie-jeebies!"

"That's Bill the bogeyman," I explained, letting the gate swing shut.

"You hurt the bogeyman?" she asked.

"He wasn't letting me in," I said.

The driveway was extra snaky today, the forest looming on all sides, mists obscuring everything. Miss Beebe put her hand in mine and pulled herself close. "I really am not happy that you've brought me here."

"Just keep it together," I said. "You really mustn't show that you're scared here."

"How come? Can the trees smell fear?"

"No, because there are things in the trees that are terrifying and you got all weird with Bill. Now suck it up."

She shoved my hand away and I took it again. "Stay close," I said.

The driveway snaked, like a black river of paving stones, around the trees and rocky outcroppings for miles, and constantly along the way there was that preternatural and unnerving silence broken only very occasionally by a snapping twig, followed by a stricken shriek of something being impaled.

I was using the flashlight on my phone to lead us through, but it was not the most reassuring light and I was certain it was a very pleasant beacon for the very real dangers stalking amongst the trees.

"Why is this here?" she asked, gesturing to the dense walls of black trunks. "Who has a forest as their garden?"

"It had to go somewhere," I explained lightly. "This is as good a place as any. Just don't go off the driveway, okay? We're safe here, but there are things that'll lure you off if they can."

In answer there was a giggle in the darkness, the giggle of a child at play. It chilled me to the bone and brought out goose-pimples up and down my arms.

"Doesn't she have visitors?" Miss Beebe asked. "I've done research, she has hundreds of people a year paying her visits for business and work."

"You shouldn't rely so much on your paperwork," I said. "Hundreds walk through those gates but only the serious get to the house. The rest get eaten."

"Eaten?"

"If they're lucky."

We continued walking, following the lit pavestones in front of us. It is a token of reality that what is real is real, and reality is a progressive system. As an example, in a nightmare you can see things that have no real presence aside from in your head – your imagination can create sweeping vistas, architecture, locations and sublime cities without needing to ever worry about building any of it. Actually within reality, it's different. *Someone* had laid these paving stones to form the decorative strips on either side of the driveway, and someone had mixed the tar and asphalt to lay this steaming yoghurt of pre-road down onto the prepared earth to create this one-way thoroughfare through this forest. I prayed they were workmen who had been Otherwise, because the idea of humans, standing in the forest, labouring away was both eerie and cruelly sad.

The forest was holding its breath, so quiet I could hear my heartbeat in my ears.

"How long have we've been walking for?" Miss Beebe asked, clinging to my arm with both hands.

"An hour?" I said. "Maybe more."

"You come here and you walk through this alone for an hour?" She sounded impressed.

"No," I said. "If you have an invite or a guide you get through faster."

"You have been invited though, I thought?"

"Yes, but you haven't. You aren't Late. The forest is testing us because of you."

"Is that possible?"

"It's quantum," I said. "I think. Or something like that, but I think it has more to do with perspective anyway. A normal sized garden can be huge given the right circumstances. Ever been lost as a child?"

"Of course."

"How big and scary does the world seem without a parent holding your hand?"

There was a very distant howl, which rumbled over the air above the trees and fell through the canopy in layers. It sounded like the biggest wolf you could imagine, but miles away. Miss Beebe clutched me closer, and frankly I was amazed I was feeling so assured. I had walked this driveway enough times to know that nothing in the forest could harm you while you were on it, but also enough times to know that the forest would do its best to get you off that hallowed path.

There was that giggling laughter again.

"What is that?" Miss Beebe demanded.

"I am not going to tell you."

The half-circle light cast from my phone fell ahead of us and revealed a bend in the driveway, a short hill of grey dirt leading up the gnarled tree roots of large, thick, almost granite-like trunks. The roots looked like bars to a prison cell window.

In front of these trees sat a little child. Her back was to us, so all we could see was the dress she had on, faded red and blue squares with a frilly collar and cute bows on the sleeves. Black hair was tied in pigtails and next to her was an old battery powered cassette radio.

Miss Beebe didn't say anything, but her grip was making my hand numb.

The child's body was making irregular jerking motions, as if she was pulling something with her arms that we couldn't see.

"Believe it or not, this could be a good sign," I said.

"Oh?"

"If this is happening now it's because we're almost at the house," I said.

The girl stopped moving when the shadow she cast in the light of the phone reached the trees. She reached out to the cassette radio with an arm that was grotesquely bloated at the forearm, with boils and pus-leaking sores. There was a withered bicep on one side and a twisted and broken hand on the other end, with a single finger ending in a ragged, rotting nail. She depressed a button on the cassette that played that childish giggle. The tape whirled for a few seconds and she pushed another button to stop it, then pushed play again and the giggling repeated.

"Whatever you do, don't run," I warned.

"Okay," Miss Beebe said.

"You'll want to, but don't do it," I said.

"Got it," she said.

"If I start running, don't let me," I said.

I kept the light on the girl because some things you want to keep in the light, but that laughing giggle coming from that cassette player was the sort of thing that monsters hide from under their beds when they hear it. This did make it impossible to hide the fact that my hand was shaking.

The child withdrew its hand and slowly rose to her feet and turned. Her face was as horribly diseased as her arm, the infection haven completely deformed what she would have called a face. A twisted mouth without any teeth hung open from a dislocated jaw. She seemed to be trying to find the source of the light, and all the while that giggling just went on and on.

"Ignore her," I said calmly. "Just walk past. She can't touch us as long as we stay on the driveway."

We took the bend slowly at a walk, while the girl hauled herself to the very edge of the driveway and, just as we passed, she ran at us with incredible speed, her little white-socked legs blurring over the short distance. I grabbed Miss Beebe's arm to stop the woman from fleeing only because it stopped me from tucking tail and sprinting in the opposite direction. But the girl stopped at the edge of the driveway and in a rage she spat, flinging pus at the invisible barrier.

We continued, following my light away from her as her screams and wails became maddening and she crashed into the vegetation.

I breathed out, relieved, before my light fell upon something in the middle of the driveway about ten feet ahead of us.

"Is that a pile of laundry?" Miss Beebe asked.

"Ah," I said. "I think that's mine."

The pile of rags and clothing stood.

"Holy cow, that's a man!" she baulked.

"Yes Vanessa," I said, drawing her behind me. "Now stay there and be a good girl."

Protect the woman, I thought to myself. Keep her behind you, because if you don't she might survive and make you look like a pussy.

The Needleman lifted itself to its full height. It spread its arms to its sides in an almost priestly, sanctified posture.

"We can't get around it," Miss Beebe whispered.

"I'm so grateful you pointed that out," I said. "I hadn't realised and could have made a really dumb mistake."

She thumped me in the ribs. "Be nice."

"Why? I'm about to be skewered!"

"*You* said nothing could hurt us in here," she hissed shrilly. "You said that we would be safe on the driveway."

"Safe from whatever is in the forest," I corrected. "It is not in the forest is it?"

"Don't be a smart-arse!"

"That was a rhetorical question," I said. "Now look, you need to go back down the driveway."

"Why?"

"Because he's here for me and I want you to be safe."

"I can help."

"I think you'll get in the way in this circumstance. He's not going to attack until you're out of the way you see, because you're not his target."

"So I can stay and help."

"Well... no," I said. "We need to get past him so I need to deal with this, but I can't if you're clinging to my arm."

"I am not leaving you," she said with firmness.

I pried her hand off my arm. "You need to. If he kills me he'll take me away with him so there won't be anything left for you to worry about, so just keep heading up the driveway until you either come to a gate or a house. Either way they'll look after you."

"Why?"

"Because they don't like hurting human women," I said.

"No... why are you insisting to fight this guy on your own?"

I looked at the Needleman, who was waiting very conscientiously for me to sort my business before conducting his own.

"Professional courtesy," I said. "Now go."

I shoved her away and for a second she looked at me hurt. Her eyes flicked from mine to over my shoulder at the Otherwise assassin standing in the way and then back to mine. She took out her phone and turned on the flashlight. "I'm going up the way but I'm watching. Don't lose, because I still need to kick your ass."

I waved her off, less interested in her symbols of solidarity and preoccupied with the monster I was facing.

"Sorry about that," I said, facing the Needleman. I turned off the phone light and slipped it back into my jacket pocket. "Ah, just before you kill me could you let my eyes adjust to the dark?"

The Needleman had not moved. The forest hadn't moved. Everything was still. Even the trees seemed to have turned to watch. Part of our training at school was getting our eyes to shift from light to night vision quickly. Night vision is more about how chemicals in the eyes react to the light but, like anything, you can train your body to adapt very quickly. It only took a couple of seconds for my eyes to get used to the shadows, in which the Needleman was just another shape.

It was black in this forest, the canopy shielding any light from the sky and the wall of trees being too dense to allow any light from anywhere else. So I closed my eyes and listened.

They had blindfolded us at school for weeks on end and made us go about our daily chores, made us fight and train without the use of our eyes. Taught us how to throw knives at targets we couldn't see and then beat us if we missed. Taught us how to intuitively sense the approach of something even when we couldn't see it and then beat us if we got it wrong.

Knowing that something is there has more to it than just your vision, they said. *Learn to use all your senses as one. Learn to perceive.*

They gave us such training when we were young, while our minds were still developing and learning about the world, and it lay down the roads of our thinking. I was as comfortable with my eyes shut as if they were open.

The other thing they taught us was that, when entering combat it is not about avoiding injury. Know that you are going to be injured, accept that there is going to be pain, do not prepare or anticipate it, just accept its promise and don't panic when it arrives.

The first needles that fired gave only the slightest *vhhiiip* as they cut through the air. In my mind's eye they shot out of the darkness following a line of sight, like a laser aimed directly for my heart and my eyes. *Take out the engine and the computer.*

Too fast and small for me to dodge them I turned to my left, shielding my heart with my body and shielding my face with my right arm, bent at the elbow like a boxer's shield.

It was like being hit by nails fired from a nail gun. The long needles hit me so smoothly that there was no pain – just a jarring impact. The pain came when the threads were pulled and I was yanked forward. My whole right side was on fire as my skin was ripped by the assassin, who was trying to pull me into a more open position so that he could make a proper kill.

This concerned me. I had entered into this with the kind of bravado, expecting to be able to fight, to throw punches and kicks and look very impressive in front of Miss Beebe, but if he was only interested in killing me it meant that he would do nothing showy or clever, he would just be as direct as tying me up in his needles and draining my blood before taking my corpse back to claim whatever reward it was expecting.

He yanked hard on the threads and pulled me off my feet, leaving me sprawled across the paving stones. Quick as I could with my other hand I reached into my pocket and found my little present. It fitted in my hand like a slab of cheese. With my right hand I swung my arm around in a broad crescent so that I gathered all the threads quickly into one bundle and pulled to measure their length and direction and, like a blind man playing darts, was able to tell exactly where they came from and hurled my present at him.

In the darkness the Needleman saw the object and reacted with a sound that made me think of a weed-whacker hitting gravel as the magnet hit him in the chest.

I heard a clinking, glassy sound of lots of pieces of metal crushing together and a gasping cry of something accustomed to having its pieces in the correct places, and then the needled threads I was holding onto went slack.

Getting to my feet, I withdrew the iklwa and followed the threads up the driveway until I my foot touched something wrapped in fabric.

"You can get anything if you know the right people," I explained. "And DHL's Late Delivery Service is incredibly efficient. That piece of metal is about as magnetised as it can get – you can thank the scientists at CERN."

I could kind of see it struggling against the magnet's pull, some of the fabric had fallen away and in the darkness there was a glint of something much blacker and shinier than merely polished metal. Nobody had seen a Needleman under its laundry and I had no intention of seeing it now. Things were usually hidden for a purpose. In the darkness I used my shoe, kicking it up its body until it found its head where it was making that wretched clicking noise. In a smooth movement that nonetheless brought fiery spikes of pain up and down my body I drove the short spear into its head.

114

Its cries became markedly more meaningful and I realised I had missed. Poor thing, it took another three tries before it finally stopped crying.

I stood, knowing that if I sat down even for a moment I wouldn't want to get up again and probed with my good hand the various points where it looked like I had been stitched. Up the driveway I saw the white light of Miss Beebe's phone bobbing up and down as she approached.

"I'm alive," I said. "But may need some help."

"Are you okay?" she asked, nearing.

"That's such a British thing to ask," I said. "'Are you okay?' I've just been in mortal combat with a bloody nightmare assassin. Now bring that light over here."

As she neared, the light brought with it a garish exposure to several things. The Needleman, through its laundry, was utterly terrifying and also, when it had fallen it had not fallen entirely onto the driveway.

The body was yanked away so fast and suddenly that it brought a scream of surprise from Miss Beebe that was immediately accompanied by a scream from me as the threaded needles suddenly whipped taut and dragged me off the driveway and into the forest.

There is no such thing as the paranormal. All of the demons and monsters of the Otherwise were called paranormal only because science hadn't gotten around to categorising them. Once something is categorised it stops being a monster, it stops being a demon. Science expands our understanding of the universe but by doing so it also limits it by boxing the wonder. It creates boundaries around our perception of things. Everything does have a scientific and even rational explanation – everything must follow the laws set for it in this physical world, and when you think you have seen something that defies these physical laws then you are mistaken.

Nothing impossible exists.

Everything is explainable. Quantifiable. Everything is measurable. In theory, this should remove the *fear* of the unknown and replace it with curiosity and wonder and feed that *need* to know and explain away the terror of the dark, of the corners. It is unquenchable if you possess it and the greatest, most impressive minds on the planet have been afflicted by this insatiable appetite to discover.

As I was dragged into the darkness of the forest, pulled by the needles hooked through my flesh, rolling around in the dirt and skidding over the ground that seemed constituted purely out of dirt, hummus and sharp rocks, I realised something. I was not one of these people.

I wasn't scared either, which surprised me frankly because I knew where I was going. Instead I was something altogether more disappointing. I was angry.

I had hoped I would prove to be one of the curious people or even one of the scared people. Curiosity and fear are signs of sharp minds. Anger in the face of danger is a sign of a brutish and blunt mind.

Whatever was dragging the Needleman was moving at incredible speed, sprinting speed, and the needles would have been torn from my flesh a lot sooner if I hadn't managed to gather them all together and hold them like I skiing rope.

Whenever something big and strong runs through a forest it naturally chooses the path of most convenience, and so I bounced off fewer rocks and collided with less trees and most of the ride was spent spraying up dirt and vegetation that whipped at my face. I may as well have been blind for all I could see though, and when we came to a stop I was met with the most sullen silence that made me aware of how much noise I must have made while crashing through the undergrowth.

I let go of the threads of the needles and my palms screamed with sticky heat. One by one I pulled out the needles that were still stuck in me and threw them to the floor. My wounds had soaked my suit and the dirt had caked over it in mud, and when I patted my sides they were dank and sticky with blood.

Swearing under my breath, the anger dulled the sharp pain that every move gave. It was like fuel for that beast inside me. I stayed where I was, sitting on my rump, looking around in the black on black. The forest smelt like a forest – trees, wood, dirt – and the silence was so solid that it screamed the presence of many, many things smart enough to be quiet and wait.

It was an intimidating silence.

How far had I been dragged? I wasn't certain. It didn't matter anyway, the forest was so crushed up that some of these trees were probably growing horizontally without realising it.

I was lucky that I hadn't broken any bones. But my ears were ringing and my skull ached from a few of the knocks I had taken as I tumbled along behind the Needleman's corpse. I tasted blood in my mouth and was running my tongue over my teeth to make sure they were all there when I sensed the first of the monsters.

They moved with a sound like cascading sand. A sound too close to a rustle to be mistaken for wind, more like a hushed whisper that flowed through the underground.

My anger slipped slightly.

They exist in the shadows.

Scientists didn't think there was anything to find in the shadows and so they didn't look very hard. But there are things that would terrify even the most rational and curious of minds. We are all afraid of the dark at some point, which is why no respected scientist would go investigating.

I pushed myself up to my feet and dusted my suit off as much as I could, brandishing the iklwa.

The rustling whispers circled around me. An auditory shark fin in the dark.

It reminded me of a colleague I knew, Katie Mercedes, a female vampire hunter who told me that vampires exist as two dimensional leeches in architecture. They were brought here from another reality, a two dimensional universe, and as such were completely flat but preferred geometric spaces. So they favoured architecture, like houses and buildings where they could haunt, almost entirely invisible, feeding off of the people living in those houses.

If you ever want to escape a vampire, run into a forest.

But know that there are worse things living there.

The dark was swarming around me. I could hear them. They're like ants, they swarm in the millions and engulf a victim, each one only large enough to take a single tiny bite – a tiny speck of flesh so small that by itself the body wouldn't even be able to bleed through it... but when a million of these bites are taken, they reduce a body into dust. Not even bones remain.

They had me surrounded on all sides, but I was still in one piece and when they stopped their rustling, their whispering, we stood in silence for almost a full minute before I cleared my throat and called into the dark, "Is that it?"

"I'm afraid not Ambassador," a voice said.

A scratching sound, the smell of sulphur, and then an orange light flared in the hand of someone I did not recognise.

He was a black man, half a foot under average height and dressed in green overalls. A tatty red baseball cap looked orange in the firelight. He had an old steel rake in one hand that he leant on like a crutch. He was chewing something, his salt and pepper jawline rotating like a cow getting through cud.

"Who are you?" I asked.

He lowered the match to a candle that was held in an iron candlestick welded to the side of the rake. The flame sparked a bit as it took onto the wick and blazed as he flicked the match out.

"I am the Gardener," he said.

I flung out my arms and groaned loudly. "Oh come off it, sir!" I shouted. "I'm almost at the end of the book! It's too late to be bringing in *another* character!"

He frowned as he considered what I had said. "Is it?"

I frowned myself, considering what I had said. "I'm not really sure," I admitted. "I take it that the forest is your garden?"

"The forest surrounds the house and is within the house's perimeter fence. It sounds like a garden to me."

I noticed that the candle flame was not flickering, although I could feel a very slight breeze. He made no effort to shield it either.

"Shouldn't I be dead by now?" I asked.

He turned his head and spat into the dark. I heard a wet slap somewhere in the gloom, then he gestured with a sidewards nod at

118

where the Needleman lay, and all that was left were a pile of metal shards and some fabric threads.

"They eat fast," I said, a little taken aback.

"They're good at keeping the place clean," the gardener pointed out. "You'd be surprised at what garbage flows in from the city. It's a big forest, close on a thousand miles across. That's bigger than the island of Britain. Things are always bigger when you look at them properly. Take for instance these ferns..."

I held up a hand. "I'm sorry, let me stop you there," I said. "I really do need to go."

"But what I have to say could be very important," he said, the candlelight glinting like starlight in his eyes. "I have walked all the mountains in this garden, raked through the grasslands, hedged the great bushes that line the bottomless gorge and cleaned the borderless ponds of–"

"Okay," I said, sharply. "Fine. What do you have to tell me?"

Awkwardly, he shuffled. "You need to ask me in the right way. I've been preparing for this, you see. It's preordained."

I went to look at my watch, but it had been thoroughly destroyed in the journey into the forest. "How should I ask?"

"With some enthusiasm would be good," he said, smiling. Aside from his perfectly straight teeth, he looked a lot like Morgan Freeman. Which could have been a cliché – I wasn't certain.

"What have you been waiting to tell m–" I started.

"No, no, no. Look... I've taken the effort to dress for the part, I've appeared out of nowhere, come on. Neither of us wants this to be a waste of time."

I put my hands on my hips and looked up. "I never knew that the forest was so well gardened," I said.

"It is a lofty task," he agreed.

"How long have you kept the garden?" I asked, squeezing the interest into my tone the same way you'd wring a sponge for every last drip.

"For longer than the city has been here," he said. "But I am but one in a long line of gardeners. We see things you would never understand, have adventures you could never conceive, have lost things you could never ascertain."

"I am in awe," I said. "Do you have a message for me?"

He sagged against his rake, his face becoming exasperated. "No! It's not a message! It's information! Nobody asked me to speak with you! It's a valuable secret that will help you on your mission!"

"Just tell me, you crazy ol–"

The lamprey slug attacked from the undergrowth, rising up behind the gardener like a giant black tongue. The size of a three seater sofa, it paused for a second behind him before belching out its innards like a pink sleeping bag that fell around the gardener and hit the ground at his feet with a wet thump. The rake fell to the side, taking the candle with it, but not before the slug followed its stomach and fell forward, folding over the struggling gardener so that its sock-like head crunched against the forest floor.

It reared up, the gardener struggling inside it, its body bulging and contorting as the man squirmed for dear life within. The slug's eyes poked out on long stalks and its tentacle snout wriggled and shook as it sniffed the air. Its dark grey flesh was the texture of phlegm, and the smell was that of the most putrid vomit.

A scream erupted from me that was reserved for frantic women. It was a scream that lifted black birds from the trees in a great cloud, it stretched my cheeks and it terrified the unsuspecting slug so much that the beast spat out the already-part-digested remains of the gardener, who unfolded into the light cast by the candle in a broken bundle, steaming with stinking gasses and slick with putrid juices. In the few seconds he had been inside the slug his skin had been digested, dissolving him right down to the bone in some places. He was most certainly dead.

What followed was a very specific chain of events that I'll always remember leaving me feeling remarkably in touch with the causality of the universe.

The gardener rolled head over heels while the slug reared up onto its foot, having established that I was suitable for its next meal. The gardener's hand flopped gracefully outwards, like a dancer in a ballet holding out a hand to be taken by a partner, yet instead it touched the candle flame of his fallen rake. It was a beautiful, loving gesture that was ruined by the slug's muscular convulsions, which would lead to it spewing out its stomach, which was, interestingly enough, lined with over thirty thousand hook like barbs that injected the most severe digestive enzymes on the planet directly into the prey the moment it was caught within that sleeping-bag stomach. The gardener's very dead fingers closed over the very alive flame.

Those digestive enzymes were also, apparently, very much oil based.

Flame exploded in a tide across the gardener's body, led by a blazing wave of blue heat that dragged a sheet of fierce yellow. The flame surged over his whole body, found the trail left from his feet to the puddle of slime surrounding the slug, and the creature – halfway through vomiting its own stomach at me – went up in a *whoosh* to suddenly becoming a twisting column of blazing fire. Panicking, it swept from side to side, trying to fling the flame off itself. The trees were suddenly ablaze, and lit up all around me the hundreds of eyes, locked within shadowy bodies, now broke their silence and flung themselves away in terror of the blazing heat that followed the trail of slime the slug had left behind it.

It brought to mind fiery dominoes.

As the slug whipped around its body it collided with trees, it rolled across the ferns and in the brush, its juices boiled and added fuel to the fire.

In great criss-crossing patterns the candle flame spread through the forest, following the path the slug had made, bringing fierce, unwanted light to one of the darkest places in the world. Slugs slept in great bundles of slime, like worms in a can, and so they were all linked intrinsically by trails of highly flammable, digestive ooze – which meant that within seconds several other slugs, each the size of household furniture and small cars, became engulfed in fire and, like this one, flung themselves around in a desperate attempt to extinguish themselves.

Eventually the fire met the dry branches of trees, and soon they found other animals living in the trees who were just as flammable and became little fire messengers.

A monster whose pigtails were on fire ran past me slapping at its head with its cassette recorder, spinning around in circles until running smack into the trunk of an ancient tree.

Gobsmacked, I stood at the centre of this all, eyes wide.

The slug nearest to me collapsed into a flaming mess, laying very still, a heap of burning snot with an audible sizzling sound, and this was accompanied by a high pitched whistling.

Quicker on the uptake than my mind, my legs turned me around and tore me into the undergrowth just as the slug exploded like a napalm bomb. Searing splatters of gooey fire flung out in all directions, setting everything they touched aflame.

I was running up the same trail that I had been dragged through, and realised it had been the slug that had dragged the Needleman off the driveway when I noticed that the flame was following me.

I leapt off the trail onto a large outcropping of rock, skidding, and fell hard on my side, but escaped the fire that shot past me in a *vooooom*. Blazing heat hit my face and my eyes as I choked on the thick smoke.

The fire trail lit my way back to the driveway, and my moment of relief was met by a moment of discovery when I realised that my suit had not been soaked with my blood after all.

Miss Beebe stared at me as I walked out of the forest, naked as the day I was born and upon a dramatic backdrop of flame. Mechanically, her arm lifted up in front of her and she took a picture of me with her phone.

"We were *that* close?" she said as the Thankeron Estate came into view around a wall of trees. We had been walking for less than a minute.

"I think the forest decided we were more trouble than we were worth," I said. I noticed she was looking back at the orange light flickering through the trees and lighting up everything. "Don't worry, the fire won't spread too far. The forest is too big for that."

She nodded, but still seemed unconvinced. "At least it's keeping you warm," she said.

At the front of the house was a crowd of people watching the blaze with spectator interest, occasionally pointing and generally just being mesmerised by the fire.

As expected, the slender man met us at the door, his smile a laceration. "You are not welcome here!" he snarled.

I had expected him to go for me but instead he went for Miss Beebe. We both acted on impulse – she kicked at the side of his thin leg, which buckled like a bread stick, and as he dropped down I drove the point of the iklwa into his grinning mouth hard enough that the blade pierced the wooden door behind him.

His legs kicked awkwardly on reflex, the polished shoes clattering against the tiles awkwardly as he was nailed at just the wrong height. Without much of a face to look surprised with, when he stopped struggling and sagged against the blade we assumed that meant he was dead.

Retrieving the iklwa from the punctured face of the slender man took a little more strength than I'd expected. I must have been angrier than I even knew when I'd smashed the spear through him in the first place – but soon enough I had it free, handing the iklwa to Miss Beebe for safe keeping. She didn't look at me as she took it, eyes still fixed with eerie fascination on the slender man as her fingers absent-mindedly closed around the weapon.

As the loathsome figure slid to a silent slouch against the door, I took Miss Beebe's hand and dragged her through the house.

"Are we going to get into trouble for that?" she asked.

"Do you care?" I asked over my shoulder as we climbed the stairs. The house had emptied, as everyone was outside watching the fire. Nobody had even noticed the slender man stuck to the door like a mosquito with a pin through its head.

"Not especially," she said. "I was just curious."

"He's a slender man," I said over my shoulder. "We'll probably get an award, a trophy... at the very least a golden star."

Madam Thankeron was waiting for us in the corridor. Dressed to impress, she looked refulgent in a brown-gold figure hugging one-piece dress, with her hair tied up in a complicated bun on top of her ever so slender neck. She gave me a long look from my toes up to my eyes and said, "I'm so very glad you dressed for the occasion. Still working out I see?"

"His clothes burnt off," Miss Beebe said. "Who are you?"

"Sorry," I said. "Miss Vanessa Beebe, this is Madam Thankeron. Madam Thankeron, this is Vanessa Beebe. Do you have any idea how much trouble I've gone through to get here?"

"I could see from my window," Madam Thankeron said.

"You don't seem too angry," Miss Beebe said. I felt her fingers tighten between mine.

"Forest fires happen all the time," the Lilith said gently. "It helps keep the slug population under control."

"Slugs?"

"The slugs are always bigger in our world," Madam Thankeron said. "You should see what the cats look like. Now, Ambassador are you ready?"

Miss Beebe stepped forward. "Hang on," she said. "Look at him. He's totally naked and still smoking. Shouldn't you get him some clothes first? What the hell is going on?"

Madam Thankeron gave me a stern look. "You haven't told her?"

I felt both their eyes suddenly upon me. The combined force of their gazes totally dulled the multitude of aches and pains I felt all over my body. Those deep bruises that deadened limbs and those fleshy scratches that burned like whip lashes — all of it faded under their scrutiny.

"I didn't think she would believe me," I said.

"And it is important that this one believes you?" Madam Thankeron asked, then to Miss Beebe added, "No offense intended."

"None taken... I think."

"And I didn't want her to try and stop me."

"Why would she try and stop you?" Madam Thankeron asked, then her expression changed and she lifted her chin, a small but indescribably sad smile spreading over her features.

Miss Beebe, scowling with anger, looked at me. "Why would I try to stop you? What are you doing?"

But I couldn't tell her. Not now – she would have definitely tried to stop me. I looked to Madam Thankeron. "Would you please inform her? I have a prior engagement I must attend to."

"Of course," Madam Thankeron said, and lifted a gloved hand to the side of my face. Her lips trembled into a sad smile and I knew she wished we were alone.

To Miss Beebe I then turned, taking her hands in mine and kissing the tops of her fingers. "Madam Thankeron will explain it all. I need you to watch my back, and protect this door."

I walked to the double doors and opened them, revealing a very large room which, like Madam Thankeron's bed chamber, was illuminated predominantly by an aquarium. This one was much smaller though, and sat in the centre of the room, only the size of a writing desk, with glass walls and an interior light. It sat on a steel table and next to it were some fresh filter pads for the interior water filter.

I took a deep breath, trying to steady my hands as I approached the tank.

Behind me, the two women walked into the room, then closed and locked the doors.

Behind me Madam Thankeron began by asking Miss Beebe a question.

"Do you know what I am?"

"You're a Lilith," she replied.

"I *am* Lilith. I was the first wife of Adam, expelled and replaced because I would not submit to him… this is how the story goes at least. I was one of the first to dance through the Garden of Eden. The first to bear one of the children of Adam."

"You said you wouldn't submit?"

"Oh, I never submitted," Madam Thankeron assured her. "I wanted to mount instead of being mounted, and I took my pleasure in the act of fornication. My own pleasure and not the pleasure of some man. This was frowned upon by God, who then made Eve. Who was more… servile."

"I didn't realise God was such a chauvinist."

"He's always been a bit of a disappointment, if I'm honest. But, he is the creator of our whole universe. This doesn't mean that he is omnipotent or omnipresent. He has all the information of the universe at his fingertips, but he doesn't care… for so long he was only interested in entertaining himself, creating planets and galaxies so that he could be worshipped. Adored. The more worship that was centred on him, the more powerful he would be, and at one stage he was very powerful indeed. Then it happened."

"What did?"

"He lost all of his power."

"Was that the apple?"

There was a pause. "No, the apple and the snake story never actually happened. No, what happened was inevitable. His creations forgot about him and he simply lost his power."

"Just like that?"

"When you believe in something it always makes it more powerful," Madam Thankeron pointed out. "The truth of something has never been important. What is important is what people believe in. Belief has real power."

I was standing in front of the tank, listening to the conversation while looking into the clear waters with their incandescent light inside. The water was still, the reflections of the light flinging up mottled shapes against the walls. It was a very simple, very basic aquarium – nothing at all impressive about it – yet it filled me with utter dread.

There was something inside the water.

"But you cannot destroy the creator of your universe, no more than a computer game could destroy its designer. Which is actually a very good analogy, and you should remember it and allow yourself to ponder it fully. So, what happened to God when he lost all of his power?"

"Did he die?"

126

"No, he reverted, and he has been like that ever since. The universe is a big place, but it is mostly unused, unwritten, undesigned. Humanity represents the source of his strength, and when we stopped believing in him he became the lowest form he was able to take. And... we've been looking after him ever since."

Miss Beebe looked at the aquarium with wide eyes. I didn't see her face, but I could have drawn the expression.

Inside the clear water was a tiny speck that shone white, bobbing along happily in little joyful puffs of its body, which was perhaps the size of an apple seed. The water wasn't as clear as I initially thought, which was of course why I was there.

I took off the top of the aquarium and put it to the side.

"Why not just let him die?" Miss Beebe asked.

"He is the source of all the energy in the universe. Don't be misled by his appearance as a happy jellyfish. If we let that creature die, God will simply be reborn. The Universe would be reset."

"That sounds... dangerous."

"Indeed. There would only be one who would survive. But who knows, he may restart the universe, flick a switch or get bored with us and just turn it off."

"But he's a jellyfish," she said.

"Nothing is as it seems, my girl. The whole universe exists in a fishbowl on a table of a being no more intelligent than any of us. A gamer, a child with a computer toy, unaware of the lives he or she could destroy. They don't care about us – but while God is trapped in that form as a jellyfish, without a brain, he is unable to escape, and therefore he's unable to kill us all. Which is why you were unable to destroy it when you came here the other night."

"I don't know what you mean," Miss Beebe said.

"Don't stress, Vanessa," I said, selecting some filters and leaning over the aquarium. "We know it was you."

"How?" Miss Beebe asked.

"Well, it could have been the butler," I said. "But I killed him coming in here, and that would be a far too anticlimactic ending don't you think? A real disappointment. You are a clear candidate for a clean and obvious villain. A character worthy of it all."

"Well, what about the barman?"

I froze halfway to the fish tank. "Bugger."

The barman stepped out of the shadows with a static frizzle and a snap of electricity that I recalled as the sound the Needleman had made. Dressed in a fitted dark navy blue suit with a pressed collar and a black tie, he looked like a gangster. The gun he was pointing at me topped the whole image down perfectly.

"Hello Donnie," he said. "Glad to see you looking so spry. Please put down the filters."

I put the filters down and leaned on the table and glared angrily at the wall for a moment. This wasn't straightforward at all — this was a complicated and twisting gnarled ball of string, with each string representing a storyline, all tying everything together, and I was being buffeted between them all. A token piece, I was barely a pawn in this game. There were so many narratives and motivations twisted in this ball, coming from me, from Madam Thankeron, from Vanessa Beebe, the barman and of course, God himself, happily bobbing around in the fish tank in front of me.

"Step away from the aquarium," he said.

I did as I was told. As long as that gun was pointed at me I would have done whatever he asked. It was strange, considering all the things that I had faced recently... the prospect of an ounce of lead hitting me at high velocity still commanded instant respect.

"I don't understand," I said.

He looked at me with exasperation. "You really haven't worked it out?"

I looked from him to Madam Thankeron and Miss Beebe. Everyone seemed to be avoiding my eye contact. I looked back at the barman. "What? Is it really *that* obvious?"

He rubbed his temples with a gloved hand, and asked with utter sincerity, "How do you manage to get through the day?"

"You're the assassin?" I asked, doggedly refusing to be sidetracked.

"Well done Donnie," he said, his tone stinking of sarcasm.

"But if you were trying to kill God, then why didn't you do it when you broke in?"

That gun hand was remarkably steady. It could have been gripped in a robotic vice. You could have balanced needles on their tips on the back of it.

"God was never the target," he said. "Besides... I like the world as it is thanks, mate. I quite enjoy the perks I have. No... my target was someone else, but I like to always add some misdirection to my contracts. It keeps people guessing."

"Who are you?" Madam Thankeron asked.

"My name isn't important," he said. "And I know the power of saying a name, so don't try to trick me Lilith. I am here to stop something terrible happening. From a universal power from being manipulated and turned into a weapon – to stop one of the darkest and most ill-trusted schools of assassins from gaining the power of a god to turn all of the universe into a slave parlour for itself."

"Why did you send the two assassins after me?" I asked.

He continued staring at Madam Thankeron and then, as if it was a great labour, he looked back at me. But his gun had never left its aim at my face. "I didn't send the assassins after you, she did."

"I did say I did," Madam Thankeron reminded me.

I folded my arms and thought about this. "So *that* part was true," I said to her. "You were testing me to see if I was able to outsmart the assassin and find them?"

She nodded, as if urging me on. But I was still thinking. I gave the barman and the front of his gun a small, embarrassed smile. "Please indulge me for a moment. I'm trying to work this out."

"Take your time," he said wearily.

The jellyfish in the aquarium bobbed merrily. Miss Beebe fiddled with her hair.

"Sooo, you know why Vanessa was given a contract for me?"

"Yes. I had no real interest in you, but when I heard the Madam Thankeron had sent an invitation to you and that Vanessa had been given a 'contract' on you, I intercepted it and delivered it myself."

"The contract?"

"No Donnie, the invitation," Miss Beebe said.

"Ah!" I said, pointing at Madam Thankeron. "So he doesn't actually work for you?"

"No. I've never met this man."

"Oh right," I said, looking back at the gun. "So you sneaked in here to test the security and to implicate me, thereby instigating Madam Thankeron in sending the Needleman for me. That gave you an excuse to come to my house and give me that protection spell, which worked for everything *except* those who have a key... so I take it you're friends with the shirime too?"

"Was," the barman said through gritted teeth. "Madam Thankeron may have recruited her but she was one of my friends. A confidante. A lover. You handed her over to an ogre."

Madam Thankeron gasped. I looked hurt. "*She* was going to eat my genitals!" I protested, then grimaced at the barman. "You said lover?"

"Yes," he said, crimson with anger.

I shuddered, made a face and went, "Ewwwww."

"After that—" the barman continued, but I held up a finger.

"Shut up," I said. "I'm working this out. Don't tell me."

He gawped at me. Miss Beebe giggled. I continued, "You guessed that Madam Thankeron would suspect me, then when she decided I was innocent, that she would then recruit me to find out who the assassin was, given my past. But why force me to come back here if I was already going to be back here? ...Ah! You knew that I wasn't going to do the favour and you needed me to say yes to it. You wanted to stop Vanessa from completing the 'contract' on me and you knew from the start that I would agree to the favour, because of the reason why Lilith asked me to do the favour in the first place?"

"Character assessments on people like you are very easy to put together," the barman asserted.

"So you knew that I would be here, you knew that I would bring the two of them here and you needed an alibi. Distracting everyone from your contract to kill my progeny by highlighting the attempt on God's life."

"Finally," he sighed.

"But why the hell make it so complicated?"

"*I* didn't," he said, his free hand pulling into a fist. "It is a simple, straightforward plan, but you're so *very* talented at making a mess of everything... oh, sod this!"

"Vanessa! Get down!"

Madam Thankeron's reflexes were lightning quick, and as the gun shifted the hand-width it took to retarget onto Miss Beebe, the Lilith had already flung herself against the blonde assassin. The gun tracking Miss Beebe like a machine, and the barman squeezed off four neat shots, by which time I had ducked and rolled towards him.

Keeping low, I went from the roll to smoothly tackling him around his leading left leg. I thrust my shoulder into the crook of his knee, bending the leg, and with my forward momentum the rest was mechanics. The leg bent, the hip twisted and the balance was lost. As far as bipeds are considered, humans are not spectacularly well equipped to stand on two legs.

He didn't follow me down, but masterfully led the motion by dropping his back leg and breaking his own fall, meaning that I trailed him by a split second. Immediately recognising the tactic, I disengaged and rolled away.

At the door Miss Beebe and Madam Thankeron were rattling the doors.

"You should be out of here by now!" I shouted.

"He's done something to the doors!" Miss Beebe shouted back angrily.

The barman grinned and slipped the gun into a holster insider his jacket. He shrugged as if to say, "*What did you expect?*" – then raised his hands up in front of himself, boxer-style.

Keep him talking...

"You want to kill the mother, don't you?"

"The mother of a hack," the barman said. "Yes. I don't think that your school should be allowed to have that kind of power. Do you?"

"Of course not," I said. "I was expelled from that school, remember?"

"So why let it happen?" he asked.

"I wasn't thinking with my head," I argued.

The barman grunted and covered the space between us with incredible speed. A barrage of punches flew at me. A jab, a cross, a hook – I dodged and shielded, parried and bobbed to save my life and landed a front donkey kick to the middle of his chest, and managed to propel myself backwards about ten feet. He was on me in a second.

He wasn't fast, but he had arms made of concrete and fists like sledgehammers and, like a sledgehammer, it isn't because it is swung fast that causes the damage, but because it is swung with meaning. Every one of his blows hurt, no matter where it hit.

I caught his left wrist with my right hand as he jammed and slammed the blade of my hand into the soft spot of his elbow joint, and I felt my hand go numb with the impact of colliding with something as hard granite.

A memory of me using that same hand to smash through bricks during a summer camp when I was thirteen sprang to mind just before I ducked under a hook that would have taken my head clean off.

This was not going well.

Guttural expletives bursting from me, I delivered ineffective kicks to the interior muscular weak points of his knees, but found the muscles to be like wood.

As far as openings were concerned he had plenty, and on an average person I'm as lethal as a hail of bullets. My punches can smash piles of bricks and my kicks can destroy baseball bats. I've shins like steel girders and knuckles like ball bearings. If the barman had been an average man he would have been wet papier mache by now.

Punches rumbled against his torso, uppercuts collided with the granite chin, kicks collided with a groin encased in iron, and when I somehow managed to weave around him and get him into a figure four headlock it was like trying to render the trunk of an oak tree unconscious.

I squeezed until my pectorals started to scream and my biceps threatened to separate from the bone and he calmly walked to the nearest wall, turned around, giving me plenty of time to decide to

132

do something else and, finally, with a resolute grunt, he ran backwards at it.

There was a solid cracking sound, like lightning, as he collided back-first into the heavy curtain and hit the glass wall of the hidden aquarium. I was the wet gooey bit in between, and as we all pressed together like a sandwich under a car tyre, a squeak escaped me.

In movies the hero carries on fighting even with broken ribs. In real life your body cannot fight if you cannot breathe.

"You are messing up my suit," the barman said, peeling my arms away from his neck and letting me drop away from him like a discarded cape. I was heaving for breath but somehow managed to stay on my feet, yet I was unable to pursue him as he strode purposefully towards the two women.

"It's a shit suit anyway," I wheezed.

He stopped and twisted his head around to look at me, a smile on his face that promised and assured me that he would make me pay for saying something so slanderous. It was a cheap shot. You never insult a man's suit unless you intend for him to be buried in it. Deeming me unworthy of his time, he turned his attention back to Miss Beebe and Madam Thankeron.

Miss Beebe looked ready to fight, but Madam Thankeron was lying down and not moving much.

"You also hit like a girl," I said. "I should have just let the women fight you. Don't know why I bothered."

"Shut up Donnie," the barman said. "You're beaten."

"Nonsense," I said. "I'm still standing and yet you're walking away from me. Is it because I'm a hack?"

"Don't be preposterous," he said. "I know the limits of your power, and they won't help you here."

But he had let me in, and there is something that you always learn quickly. People who like to fight, who are good at fighting, like to talk too. I've never met a man who enjoyed fighting who didn't enjoy a good chinwag. It was like foreplay before sex, antipasti before the main course.

"Are you sure? Because you're still walking away from me." I pushed away from the aquarium, slapping my thighs theatrically. Everything hurt but it didn't matter if he couldn't hear it from my voice. "You're lucky too. I would have had you out of the suit and taken your cherry. Not a pleasant thing but I think you'd have liked it."

That's the other thing — a man covered in tattoos, who talks a mean talk and wears a mean suit. It's about making a statement. Statements are like good architecture, it's built to be seen and admired. His statement was one of a domineering uber-man. You could tell it in everything he did. This was a man who had never tried anything different, and so believed he was straight by default. Calling a big bloke with tattoos gay is like a teenager with a can of spray-paint besmirching your big building.

He stopped mid-stride.

I choked out a laugh. "I don't believe it, you're homophobic in this day and age? Come on big man, it's cool. As long as you don't shag animals it's fine, hell in Norwich they have a reputation for family reunions."

He turned around.

"You look like you'd be a taker rather than a giver anyway, so why don't you just come here and bend over and we'll get star— *oh bugger!*"

His tackle put his shoulder right in my guts. My insides spasmed together into twisted ribbons of tissue and we bounced off the aquarium, tearing the curtain off its rail, and went sprawling onto the ground.

"You calling me a faggot boy?" he roared, tearing the curtain to pieces around us as if he wanted to get the spray of my blood as well spread as possible. "Or are you just a fucking stupid arsewipe who doesn't know what the fuck he's talking about, you little shitting faggot?!"

One of his mighty hands grabbed the front of my skull and his fingers crushed into my head.

"Get on your knees, you weaselly ponce!" he spat, lifting me up to my knees. "You surprised that it all ended up like this?

"I often surprise myself," I wheezed, as the lights started going out. "But before I forget... you dropped your gun."

Sometimes when you're really angry you get tunnel vision. Winning a fight is all about picking the right target at the right time in a storm of injury and pain. I held the gun out at the nearest target in front of me and squeezed off several shots.

Like a sea sponge exploding during breeding season, his crotch erupted as the bullets tore through the soft tissue. He buckled and dropped me to clutch at what was left between his legs, as if he thought he could will them back into existence with his touch.

Staggering a couple of pained steps backwards, he screamed while I changed hands of the gun to my right hand and supported it properly with the left, then aimed and fired a bullet through one of his knee caps. The bullet hit him just on the side of the patella and he twisted over and fell heavily, shaking and swearing, veins causing the tattoos in his neck to dance.

"You're a tough one," I said, once again getting to my feet. "But people don't see things that aren't a threat and you always choose a weapon that could hurt you the most."

Red faced, his eyes bulging, veins sticking out of his neck and face, he wasn't going to give me a handy reply.

I aimed again and emptied the remainder of the magazine into his eye socket. Then, when I ran out of bullets, I stuck the barrel of the gun into the minced mess and stamped on it as hard as I could.

"Was that necessary?" Miss Beebe asked.

I spread my arms. "Look at me!"

Miss Beebe tried to help me but I waved her off. Everything hurt so much I didn't want anyone to touch me again. I limped to where Madam Thankeron lay. The woman was looking annoyed.

"I hate scars," she said, digging into a hole in her side until she pulled out a bullet. "I believe you have a job to do?"

I looked at Miss Beebe. "Will you help me? This job will need some finesse."

"Of course," she said, and together we walked back to the tank.

The tiny jellyfish inside was merrily plopping its way through the murky water looking for its colleagues.

As we worked, Miss Beebe said, "It is strange isn't it? You have the fate of the universe in your hands."

"Hmmm," I said.

"Every religion and faith is wrong," she said.

"Not quite," I said. "They say that God made man in his image. We just got the timing a bit wrong. Besides, didn't you understand what Madam Thankeron said? It's all like a game… we're just… game pieces."

"You seem remarkably fine with it all?"

"It's been an emotional couple of days," I said. "It's all still absorbing."

Changing the filters took all of ten minutes.

"There," I said. "Job done. A bit anticlimactic isn't it?"

"What is special about this water anyway?" Miss Beebe asked.

"Nothing really," I explained. "Fragile jellyfish need specific water and any other water could be toxic to it."

"Like the water in the aquarium?"

"Precisely."

"Right."

There was a long creaking crunching of glass and fibres that stretched across the entire room and echoed elsewhere in the house, like the spreading song snow makes on a mountain seconds before an avalanche flattens villages and wraps things around trees.

We all looked at the floor to ceiling aquarium with the hundreds of thousands of gallons of water in it. Like all things in Norwich, space was crunched. There were whales and other monsters that lived in there.

Streams of water leaked out and splashed onto the floor and the three of us splashed through it as we wheeled the aquarium across it towards the doors.

Madam Thankeron rattled the doorknobs, trying to open them, and I shouted at her to get out of the way and threw as much body weight as I could against the door panels… and bounced off.

"Oh get real!" Madam Thankeron muttered. "Volka! Jetson!"

The hounds erupted from the shadows, snarling and roaring. Miss Beebe saw them and screamed.

"You could have called them when the barman was pummeling me!" I snarled as we pushed the aquarium out of the way. The water was now ankle deep. Madam Thankeron ignored me and commanded her hounds to bash down the door, and the pair of beasts bounded through the water, all muscle and hair. They turned the panels of wood to little more than smouldering toothpicks.

"I couldn't call them!" she said. "They're anticlerical!"

"What does that mean?" Miss Beebe asked, helping me push the aquarium through the water and the doorway. The jellyfish had made its way to the edge of the glass for a better view.

"They're *hell* hounds," I said, slapping my forehead.

"Meaning?"

Seconds later the three of us were racing down the corridor, pushing the aquarium in front of us, pursued by two gigantic, hell-enraged hounds desperate to destroy the god creature they could sense within the aquarium – and then just behind them a wall of water containing many things with fins, tentacles and teeth wanting to eat whatever they could find.

The stairs at the end of the corridor were fast approaching. The stairs that lacked a banister – those goddamn artsy, decoratively dangerous stairs! I picked a door along the corridor wall at random, opened it, swung the aquarium, Miss Beebe and Madam Thankeron into it and banged it shut just as the hell hounds reached us, avoiding their snarling maws by heartbeats. Their savage, hellish roars ended with surprised wet yelps as a wall of water collided with them.

We backed away from the door panel as it bulged inwards, mucky brown water leaking in around the edges.

"It's a strong door, but it won't hold," Madam Thankeron said.

I spun around and took a quick sweep of the surroundings. It was a guest room, a huge gothic iron bedspread with four posts holding a massive white mattress. The bed linen was folded up in the centre. Two chocolates were on the pillows.

One of the walls was a giant pane of glass overlooking an Asian cityscape. Miss Beebe was staring out at it in confusion.

"Not all rooms are next to each other," I said quickly, rolling the aquarium to the far side of the room and wedging it out of the way against the wall. "This room is still in Madam Thankeron's estate, technically. Just with a better view."

While Miss Beebe looked at the view of a city lit up from within with an electro-neon light from what must have been one of the higher sixty storey windows, the bedroom door was bulging as more of the oceans within Madam Thankeron's aquarium spilled out. There was no longer a roar though, meaning the corridor was thoroughly flooded. I splashed through ankle deep water and pushed the mattress off of the bed frame. It splatted wetly across the other end.

"What are you doing?" Madam Thankeron asked, as she took Miss Beebe gently by the shoulders and guided her to where I had stowed the smaller aquarium. Inside, the jellyfish was dancing with its reflection.

"Erm," I said, wishing I could sound a bit more confident. "Something really stupid I imagine."

Both women watched me while I hauled the aquarium across the room to the built in wardrobe on the far end with the mirrored walls, which showed just how ridiculous a naked man can look while dragging an aquarium.

Madam Thankeron sloshed through the water to help me lift the aquarium into the closet.

"Okay, this makes sense, but it does look like you're planning to throw that bed through the window?"

I laughed as I positioned the wrought iron bed spread in the centre of the room with its edge facing the window. "Does it? Hand me the iklwa."

Almost seeming to forget she'd been given it after the slender man incident, Miss Beebe passed me the weapon, her expression riddled with quizzical anticipation. With the iklwa in hand I went to the window and knocked on the glass with my knuckles, conscious at every moment that the water in the room was getting deeper and that my plan, if you could call it that, had one very, *very*, serious flaw, which I was resolutely ignoring.

138

"That is double pane glass," Madam Thankeron said.

"Least of my problems," I sang merrily. I continued rapping my knuckles on the glass until finding what I was looking for and, holding the iklwa in both hands, I rammed the spear tip against the glass with as much might as I could muster.

I was rewarded with a chip.

"Thank God, we're saved," Miss Beebe said sarcastically where she knelt in front of the door, padding the bottom of it with the bed linen.

Turning the iklwa around, I used the edged bottom of it and, with both hands, I used it like a pick and slammed it into the chip. When that didn't work I crouched in the water, surprised by how deep it had got in the past few seconds, and with the iklwa over my head I hammered it with as much leverage as I could. The answering crack didn't even make a sound — it just appeared through the glass, all the way through to the other side.

"Get into the cupboard with Vanessa," I told Madam Thankeron.

The tall woman waded to me and drew me up, kissing me hard on the lips. Her mouth was hot and her tongue fierce. Looking me in the eyes she said, "You are a giant amongst men."

She climbed into the closet.

Miss Beebe grabbed my head and kissed me, her tongue wrestling mine as fiercely as it had done earlier. She looked me in the eyes and said, "You're the best man I know."

Then she climbed into the closet.

Once they were safely stowed away, I braced myself behind the bed frame and, with as much strength as I could summon, aimed its corner at the crack in the window. I expected to have to try this at least twice.

The bed frame no doubt caused a lot of damage and trouble when, after a long and graceful fall, it collided with the ornamental promenade that was one of the prides of the Five Lotus Blossom Hotel, which boasts rooms with the most exquisite views of Kuala Lumpur. Unlike in films where falling debris is usually spotted by a convenient woman who can scream a warning, in real life when hearing screams, people tend to not immediately look up. Miraculously, despite this, the bed frame didn't kill or injure anyone. Even the water that poured out of the window above like a vast murky waterfall had enough height to dissipate into a fine but drenching rain. Indeed, what was responsible for the casualties, and there were many, was that given the sudden tide created when the rising water was able to gush out over the lip of that broken window wall, the door to the room succumbed to the added pascals and ripped clean off its hinges. The current created tore not only water, but animals, fish, mer-creatures and straight up monsters through the bedroom door, swirling them briefly around the room like miniatures caught in the tide of a flushing toilet bowl, tearing picture frames from the walls and furniture from the floor and flinging it all together out of the empty space while I clung to the curtain.

"Aaaaaaaaaaaaa!" I screamed.

The tide ended as the water ran out and I managed to, by my fingers and toes, clamber back into the room. Once on the carpet I crawled as fast as I could away from the window to get into the safe crevice of the apartment. Cold wind whipped at my body and I kept to the walls because they offered some kind of security. Wading through ankle deep water, I made my ponderous way to the back of the room.

"Girls!" I called, because in the panic I had forgotten both their names. "Are you okay?"

I tripped along the way over the stranded and desperately flailing body of a
fish, which looked up at me with pleading eyes – right up to the point where I kicked it out the window.

"We're still alive, so I assume the jellyfish is still in its tank?" I shouted as I got to the cupboards and, bracing myself for what I was going to find, I pulled the doors open. "It would be nice if you answered me!"

I saw both of them and instantly knew what was happening. "Seriously?" I asked, hands spread. "I'm out here fighting for the universe and you're in here..." – I turned my head to the side to get a better look – "...doing that. Bit much isn't it?"

From the entanglement of limbs that was so tastefully cast in partial shadow by the light of the tank's smaller aqua blue light, a hand reached out and took hold of me and drew me into the cupboard.

I pulled the door shut behind me.

SIXTEEN

At the party, there were enough mirrors to make you think you were living in a disco ball. Huge polished panels of metal and glass in gaudy frames positioned all around the vast dining hall gave the unnecessary illusion that there were more people in attendance than were in attendance. The guests were crowded in so close that I was able to fish bits of conversation from each group of people as I drifted through. Armed with champagne and a nefarious purpose, my intentions were less than noble and attentively focused on the number of female lingerie models who were present and, in part, the centre of this little party.

This particular event had drawn in designers, artists, models and media from around the country, and my recently appointed personal assistant had mentioned in passing that there were guests who were Otherwise and Late as well as human.

"Recently appointed," was an interesting way of putting it. Basically, the day after returning from Malaysia, I had been rudely awakened by a knock at the door to find a woman standing there with an iPad and the expression of someone who is accustomed to scheduling. She had then proceeded to tell me that her name was Danielle and she was my personal assistant, also that I had three meetings that day and would have to dress to suit. I also now had an office and, what was worse, office hours.

I didn't know if I was being rewarded or punished.

I had lost my bearings in the crowd and took a moment to figure out where I was. The mirrors, some of them the size of bus fronts, were offering far too many distractions in the large hall, with its curving Roman archways and thick granite pillars. But I deduced I was near the buffet table and, like a shark spotting a floundering seal, I changed direction and headed that way.

Hovering around were the models, wrapped up like presents in their silk gowns, waiting to be called to the catwalk and in the meantime hovering near, but just out of reaching distance of, the overloaded buffet.

As I neared, I heard some of them daring each other to eat an olive. My eyes fixed on the rear of one of them. She was a tall slinky girl, with small shoulders and intensely curly red hair. Her pale calves poked out from under the branded black silk gown, and the subtly athletic movement of her calf muscle had me biting my lip.

I fixed my best smile and was taking a breath to speak when, quite suddenly, everything in the hall went silent.

I spun full circle, expecting to see what had caught everyone's attention and stopped the conversation, and discovered I was in a crowd of mannequins. They weren't real mannequins, but everyone had just stopped moving and was frozen in place.

From face to face, everyone's film had been paused and I would have laughed at some of their expressions if not for the annoyance I felt.

I finished my drink and balanced the glass on the top of a bald businessman who was frozen halfway through showing a group of people how to strut.

"You have my attention," I said into the stillness.

"Of course you do," a vaguely familiar voice said at my side.

The person who stood there was so out of place that my annoyance was shunted aside. "Keith?"

The taxi driver gave a happy wink and said, "I have a favour to ask of you."

COMING SOON –

That Time I Wrestled With The Woman Who Killed Monsters With Her Bitey Vagina

(A Working Title)

There are centaurs in Purgatory, and war is brewing.

Donnie Rust has a new office, new responsibilities and a new personal assistant who *really* doesn't like him. There is a lot to learn about the city of Purgatory, and he is just discovering that what goes bump in the night may also have teeth and, potentially, an audience.

The most irresponsible public servant in the world returns in the second instalment of his Working Title series, as he tries his best to uncover 'whodunnit' before war breaks loose and even more people die and, perhaps worst of all, he gets blamed for it.

Printed in Great Britain
by Amazon